I0609457

POISON AND PUDDING

A SEASIDE FRENCH PATISSERIE MYSTERY
BOOK 2

KAT BELLEMORE

KB PRESS

CHOOSE YOUR OWN ADVENTURE: MYSTERY OR ROMANCE

MADDIE SWALLOWS MYSTERIES:

New Mexican Cozy Mystery

Dead Before Dinner

Dead Upon Arrival

Dead Before I Do

Dead Among Stars

Dead by Design

Dead in the Dark

Dead Without a Hitch

SEASIDE FRENCH PATISSERIE MYSTERIES

Death and Dacquoise

Poison and Pudding

Bullets and Beignets

BORROWING AMOR: New Mexican Romance

Borrowing Amor

Borrowing Love

Borrowing a Fiancé

Borrowing a Billionaire

1

Something was burning.

No smoke alarms had gone off, but I had the nose of a basset hound, and it was never wrong.

I blindly felt for my glasses on the nightstand and slipped them on. The digital clock claimed it was four-thirty, but I never trusted technology. Same reason I didn't own a cellphone.

The stars were still out and the moon high above the ocean, so the clock might be right this time. Hopefully our volunteer firemen could be wakened at this early hour. Their main job was keeping watch on the bonfires that people started on the beach each evening, and even then, they'd never had to actually intervene before. I wondered if they even knew how to put out a fire. Maybe "fireman" was more of an honorary title.

"Dottie," I yelled. "Something is burning."

I pushed myself out of bed and hoped she'd heard me. A normal person, if they suspected their home and business was on fire, wouldn't bother changing out of their pajamas—not even taking the time to put on a robe. Every second counted. And yet, before I realized what I was doing, I'd started to throw on a pair of slacks and a blouse. My mother had instilled a habit of strict discipline into my sisters and me, and before I'd thought better of it, I had already begun changing. I frowned, annoyed at myself, but at this point, it would have taken longer to undo what I'd already done.

"Dottie," I called again as I fastened the last button.

"I'm coming," she grumbled from the next room. "Can't find my cane."

Dottie was my older sister by three years, and we'd recently celebrated her seventieth birthday. Before we'd moved to Starlight Ridge a year and a half earlier, her health had been on a downward trajectory, which wasn't all that unusual for retirees. That didn't make it any less frustrating. Since moving to this little Californian coastal town, however, we'd both become stronger and had more energy than we'd thought possible. I attributed it to the sun, the fresh salty air, and the parkour class we'd recently begun to attend.

That cane, though—Dottie didn't need it nearly as much as she thought she did, and yet she couldn't let it go.

"If our shop burns down today of all days—" I started.

Dottie cut me off as she exited her room. "That's not going to happen. I won't allow it."

I doubted that Dottie had any control over if our bakery was destined to become a pile of ash, and I wished I shared her confidence in its chances of survival. Especially because we'd been working so hard in preparation for this weekend.

I took in Dottie's attire, and I had to stifle a groan. My sister was also dressed in slacks and a blouse. Thanks, Mom. If today was the day we died, we'd curse your strict discipline all the way to the grave.

"Autumn has been baking for nearly twenty-four hours straight," I said as I moved toward our apartment's front door. "I told her to go home early last night and get some sleep, but she refused."

Dottie beat me to the staircase that led from our apartment to our bakery, but then took her time stepping down to the first step. The steep staircase didn't have a handrail, and I'd told Dottie we needed to make it a priority, but she'd insisted we focus on other things.

Making it through our first tourist season, for one.

I tapped my foot impatiently and considered calling the fire chief while I waited. We'd already wasted enough time changing clothes in the middle of the night. At least we hadn't worried about hair or makeup. Our mom wouldn't have been caught dead without her magenta lipstick. At this rate, that was where we were headed. Dead without our lipstick. There were worse things.

"I'm doing the best I can," she grumbled.

I thought she probably believed that, but it wasn't true. "Just a few months ago you practically jumped down these steps when Autumn was in trouble with the sheriff. But now that our shop is in trouble, you've suddenly decided you're going to take extra precautions?"

Dottie tossed me an annoyed glance. "The steps are steep."

As she paused to massage her knee, her cat, Skittles, wandered out of Dottie's bedroom. The tabby stretched and glared at me like it was my fault she'd been woken up. She then raced past Dottie and bounded down the stairs.

"Showoff," Dottie muttered.

"You could learn a thing or two from Skittles," I said. "That cat has no fear."

Dottie grumbled about how I couldn't compare the two but seemed to have a quicker step as she continued her descent.

When Dottie reached the final step, Autumn appeared at the bottom of the staircase, scaring Dottie so badly that she nearly fell off of it. Thankfully, Autumn had amazing reflexes and managed to catch her in time.

"I'm so sorry to have woken you," Autumn said, holding on to Dottie until she was certain that my sister had regained her balance. "The smoke is my fault. This weekend has had me all tied up in knots. I know most people probably won't be thinking about where they can buy French pastries—they're here for the surfing. But we have to be prepared. I must have dozed off, though, because one minute I was waiting for the bread pudding to finish, and the next, smoke was pouring out of the oven." After seeing our alarmed expressions, she hurriedly added, "I turned everything off and propped open the back door, so no harm done, other than the inedible bread pudding."

She paused.

"The smoke alarms in the kitchen should have activated and woken me up. You did check them to make sure they were up to date when you restored the bakery, didn't you? It's part of the safety inspection you received."

Dottie glanced up at me, and I gave her a guilty look in return.

"A couple weeks after the inspection, one of the detectors started chirping because of a low battery," Dottie said, turning back to Autumn. "I didn't have any batteries on hand and couldn't tell which one was chirping, so I turned each one off as I searched for the culprit, and wouldn't you know it, it was the last one I tried."

"And you didn't turn the others back on," Autumn guessed.

Dottie nodded. "It has been on our list of things to take care of."

What she didn't say was that it had been on my list of responsibilities, and I had dropped the ball. It had just moved up to priority number one, though, and I'd make sure it was remedied by the end of the week. I'd have our local handyman, Davis, take care of it.

"It's my fault," I confessed. "Are you all right?"

She gave a little nod. "Yes, I'm fine. I'll just redo this last batch of—"

"No, you won't," Dottie interrupted. "You shouldn't be so tired that you're falling asleep in the kitchen. Hang up your apron and go home. We won't be opening until after noon anyway. Jo and I have never been to a surfing competition, and we'd like to see what all the hubbub is about."

"You and the rest of the town," Autumn said. "I've never seen people as excited as they are for this weekend."

Every summer Starlight Ridge was flooded with tourists who wanted to hike and see the local wildlife, mostly the turtles and dolphins, as well as get a taste of our colorful shops and pristine beaches.

But this weekend—no one in Starlight Ridge had experienced what this surfing competition would bring. Thanks to one of the country's biggest surfing competitions choosing our little town for this year's festivities, we were about to be inundated with more people in one weekend than we usually saw all summer.

"Can you blame them, when our lifeguard is one of the main contenders?" I asked. "I'm sure Isaac is freaking out. He's become a kind of local celebrity, everyone coming out to cheer him on."

I was nervous for him just thinking about it.

"We've all surfed together since we were children," Autumn said, "but never in an environment like this. Never with all these people watching, and Isaac is going to have the hopes of all of us locals resting on his shoulders while he's out there. It sounds awful." She stifled a yawn, and I saw just how dark the bags under her eyes had become. "That's all while having to compete against Bryce Carlton."

I had made my way down the stairs, and I squeezed past where Dottie stood, leaning against the wall for support. "Yes, Isaac has mentioned him to me on more than one occasion. But Isaac isn't who I'm worried about right now. You need to go home, Autumn. You won't forgive yourself if you miss seeing Isaac compete tomorrow because you couldn't stay awake."

"Technically, it's today," Dottie said, stifling her own yawn.

Autumn looked like she wanted to protest as I steered her toward the front door, but she was ultimately too tired to do so.

I knew how she felt.

This summer had been the first tourist season Dottie and I had experienced, and there were times we'd wondered if we'd make it. We were at the tail end of it now, the surfing competition signaling the beginning of our off season.

I still couldn't believe we'd uprooted our lives and opened a bakery at our ages.

Our eldest sister had lived in Starlight Ridge and owned Sandcastle Souvenirs. When she'd been murdered a couple of years earlier, Dottie and I had decided to move out here and take over. Even though both of us had already been retired, it had seemed the right thing to do.

Instead of selling clearance-item souvenirs, however, we'd decided to restore her shop to the bakery it had previously been. Never mind that neither of us knew how to bake—we'd hired Autumn to take care of that. She'd learned to bake when she'd lived in Paris and only knew how to bake French pastries, but I preferred it that way. It made us unique, and as it turned out, all my favorite pastries were French.

We'd underestimated how much work went into owning a business, however. We'd been open only a few months and it had already taken its toll. A six-month nap would be required to help us make it through the next tourist season. And that was assuming we somehow managed to make it through the next two days.

"The first round of the competition starts in only a couple of hours," Dottie said from the stairway as I said goodbye to Autumn and relocked the front door. "If I crawl into bed now, I'll never make it back out."

I agreed, and so we put ourselves to work, packaging up the pastries that Autumn hadn't been able to. I fully expected that by lunchtime, our little bakery would be flooded with surfing spectators, and like Autumn, I wanted to be prepared.

If we'd known that there wouldn't be a second round to the competition, we might not have gone to so much trouble.

2

D espite the lack of sleep, adrenaline buzzed through me. Dottie and I didn't bother driving down to the beach because the road in front of our shop was already lined with the cars of spectators who couldn't find parking at the boardwalk.

The excitement in the air was palpable, hundreds of people surrounding us at every turn. We were by far the oldest ones there, but I didn't mind. It would make us seem like the cool grandmas that everyone wished were theirs.

"Do you see Isaac?" I asked Dottie, my gaze scanning the beach. I held a little box that I'd tied up with some red string. "I want to give him this bread pudding and wish him good luck. He told me once that he doesn't eat breakfast, but he's going to need the sustenance if he's going to do his best out there."

The problem was that most of the men were wearing

either tank tops or no shirt at all, and as my gaze swept over the sea of onlookers, they all blended together. Individually, they looked different, but all clumped together like this? It was impossible.

Dottie's gaze scanned the area before settling on a spot directly in front of us. She pointed. "There he is. He's talking with another surfer. At least, I think it's another surfer. I can't tell who's competing and who's just here to watch."

"We should have brought chairs," I said, wondering how long a surfing competition usually lasted.

Dottie laughed. "You think we could have carried chairs all the way from the bakery? We were lucky to get ourselves here."

"Speak for yourself," I said, frowning. The walk hadn't even winded me. Mostly.

"Oh, don't be like that," she said. "So what, we don't have the stamina we had in our twenties. It's not a bad thing—just a fact of life."

For some people, maybe, but I was determined to defy expectations. And if no one else needed chairs, neither did we.

"Jo. Dottie," someone called from our right. We turned to see Jessie, our friend and the matriarch of Starlight Ridge. She wasn't much younger than us, and yet she appeared to have the energy of a fifty-year-old. That was my ultimate goal. To defy age. She waved us over and pointed to the ground next to her feet.

Camping chairs, still folded.

Thank goodness.

"You go ahead," I said. "Save me a spot. I'm going to run this bread pudding over to Isaac."

I should have read the situation first but was oblivious as I made my way through the crowd.

By the time I reached Isaac and his friend, I'd already called his name, waving the pudding in the air so he'd see I'd brought treats.

I hadn't noticed the anger rolling off the pair. Hadn't noticed the narrowed eyes and frowns. I slowed to a stop, wondering if it was too late for me to walk backwards, melt into the ground, and pretend I'd never been there.

"Hey, Jo," Isaac said, turning to me, his voice cheerful, though a storm still brewed in his dark eyes. It was a sharp contrast to his usual easygoing nature. Unlike the typical Californian surfer, he had a dark complexion and even darker hair, like he might have migrated over from Hawaii. All the women in town went crazy for him, but he usually shrugged it off. He didn't care about any of that.

The only things Isaac cared about were the things that could get him closer to the water. And surfing trumped them all.

"Hi," I said uneasily, then held up the box of bread pudding. "Just thought I'd wish you good luck and give you a little something from the bakery. Not that you need the luck, of course."

The other man snorted. "He needs all the luck he can

get." His lips widened into a grin, and he extended a hand to me. "I'm Bryce Carlton. You probably recognize me from all the posters."

I didn't know what posters he was talking about, but I did know the name Bryce Carlton.

"I'm sorry, I don't," I said, taking his hand. "Your name is Brian, you say? It's lovely to meet you. Are you here to cheer Isaac on, as well?"

The look on Bryce's face was one that I'd be able to carry with me whenever I was having a bad day and needed a good laugh. No camera needed. The shock in his face—as if I really thought he was a lowly spectator and not one of the highest-ranking surfers in the competition. As if I hadn't heard about the scandals, accusations swirling that he had cheated or paid off the judges for higher scores.

I merely smiled, like I didn't notice.

Bryce spluttered for a few seconds before yanking his hand back.

"No, I'm not," he said, then turned his gaze on Isaac. "We're going to settle this on the waves, and you're going to wish the competition hadn't come to you—that you hadn't been humiliated in front of every neighbor you have, every friend. After we're done this weekend, they won't be able to look at you without feeling sorry for you."

I frowned. "Well, that's not a very nice thing to say."

Bryce threw me an annoyed glance and then stalked off.

Isaac released a heavy sigh, like the conversation with Bryce had taken all his energy and he didn't have any left to give.

I rested a hand on his arm. "Don't you give that man another thought. You do what you do best, and the universe will take care of the rest."

Isaac gave me a weak smile. "Thanks, Jo. But what if my best isn't enough? Rumors have circulated for years that Bryce is somehow cheating, but no one can figure out how."

Poor Isaac. He looked so dejected at the thought that no matter how well he or the other surfers performed that day, they didn't have a chance.

He gave me a little wave and wandered off, probably to mentally prepare himself for what was to come.

It was only then I realized I was still holding his bread pudding. "Wait, you forgot—" I called, but I'd already lost him in the crowd.

What was I going to do with this pudding?

I scanned the beach as I made my way toward where Jessie and Dottie had disappeared.

"Jo!"

My gaze landed on Jessie, who was waving her arms a little farther down the beach. They already had the chairs set up and the food out. This was my kind of day.

And not far from her was Bryce Carlton. He had settled himself on an upside-down bucket and was waxing his board, though it seemed to be more of a calming strategy. He wore a fierce expression, and he seemed to be putting all of his frustration into the rhythmic motion. He was surrounded by cameras and several women who appeared to be adoring fans, but he didn't so much as glance their way, his entire focus on his board.

I waved to Jessie so she'd know I'd seen her and then walked over to Bryce.

Over the past year, I'd found that bribery with pastry could go a long way, whether it was getting the local pastor to shorten his sermons or getting an extra card at bingo.

I doubted surfers were any different.

"Hello, Bryce Carlton," I said, approaching him. As I drew close, I saw that his board had a giant illustration of a manatee on it.

Bryce glanced up, and a mixture of emotions crossed his face. Surprise. Confusion. Maybe even a little annoyance.

He grunted and turned his attention back to his board.

"I wanted to apologize," I said. "I feel that you and I may have gotten off on the wrong foot. You see, the only exposure I have to surfing is our local kids who go out every day. Isaac has always been the most committed. He's quite good, you know. But I understand that you are very talented yourself, and I brought a peace offering, if you'll accept it."

I held it out to him.

He didn't take the pastry box from me, instead eyeing it

with suspicion. I supposed that made sense, considering I was friendly with his rival.

"It's not poisoned. Just some bread pudding from the bakery that my sister and I own. A goodwill gesture." Several of the cameras had turned toward me, and I was unsure if I was meant to acknowledge them. I gave a little wave, then turned back to Bryce. "You should try it. Our pâtissiere studied in Paris, so you know she's good. The Paris that's in France. Not Idaho."

"There's also a Paris in Kentucky," a young woman said, stepping forward. "That's where I'm originally from." She was a classic type of beautiful. I could never pull off the bikini she wore, but what I loved most were the pink streaks in her short blonde hair. Mostly because they matched mine. She had long pink fingernails that were the same shade. They had glitter on them, and I was immediately envious. "Even if Bryce won't take your gift, I'm happy to accept it for him."

I grinned, liking her already. "You have a beautiful accent," I said, and handed her the pastry box. "My name is Jo."

"I'm Felicity," she said, and lifted the lid, inhaling deeply. She turned to Bryce. "Are you really not going to eat this? Because it smells divine."

He didn't bother even glancing at her but waved a hand through the air, as if to say he didn't care one way or the other.

"One of the perks of being his girlfriend," she said,

lowering her voice as if we were in on a secret together. "When he's in the zone, nothing else matters. And that means I get all the gifts he doesn't want. Which, from this point until the end of the competition, is everything."

Girlfriend. Interesting. I could work with this. Maybe she'd let slip how Bryce was cheating in his competitions and I could help level the playing field for Isaac. Except, she'd never say anything she shouldn't with all these cameras around.

"I hear he's quite a good surfer," I said, keeping my voice equally low. I nodded toward where Dottie and Jessie were watching us, their expressions curious. "Would you like to join us for a few minutes? We have plenty of food, and I'd love to get the name of your hairdresser. I dye my own hair, but it doesn't always turn out." I tousled my own dyed hair. "Our shade matches, doesn't it?"

I didn't have the skill to streak my hair, so it always ended up one color. I'd tried all sorts of colors, from purple to blue to green—green had been a mistake. But I always came back to pink.

Felicity laughed. "I think my hairdresser is a bit too long of a drive for you, but I'd be happy to give you some tips." She turned to Bryce. "I'm going on a walk. Be back in a bit." He barely acknowledged her, a slight nod the only indication that he'd heard her.

Felicity stepped away but then paused, as if she'd forgotten something. She called to him over her shoulder, "Don't forget to eat your oatmeal. It's sitting on top of the cooler. It has extra berries today—you're going to need the energy."

He didn't respond.

"The zone," she whispered to me with a knowing look, and then she followed me over to where Dottie and Jessie were still watching us. "Honestly, it's lucky you came along with this delicious bread pudding or I'd be forced to eat oatmeal for breakfast, as well. Not my favorite."

The cameras remained where Bryce was waxing his board—something I had been counting on. They didn't care about the girlfriend. All except one. A woman who looked like she must be a reporter, considering her pantsuit, had just walked up and joined the crowd, but then had paused, watching Felicity and me. She whispered something to her cameraman and nodded in our direction. When I met her gaze, she glanced away.

"Bryce is quite famous, isn't he?" I said, turning back to Felicity as we walked.

Felicity gave a vigorous nod. "Oh, yes. Everyone just adores him."

It seemed there was a case of rose-colored glasses going on here, or maybe Felicity only surrounded herself with people who truly did love Bryce Carlton.

"How did he become so good?" I asked, unsure how anyone would even go about cheating while surfing. You either stayed on your board or you didn't.

A shirtless man walked by just as I asked the question,

and he glanced back at Felicity and me with a crooked smile. "Bryce got so good by watching me."

Felicity smirked. "You wish, Richards."

He must have been one of the competing surfers. A large tattoo covered his right arm—a skeleton on a surfboard.

The surfer's smile grew. "You just wait and see who wins this little shindig. You're finally going to leave Bryce and be with a real surfer for once."

"You and I both know that you don't stand a chance against Bryce."

The skeleton surfer's lips dipped, and he stalked off.

"Another rival?" I guessed.

Felicity nodded. "Michael Richards. The bad boy of surfing. If there is a stereotype, he tries to break it, even to his own detriment. It's why he'll never be the best—he's too worried about his image and not worried enough about improving his skill." She tore her gaze away from Michael's retreating figure and linked her arm through mine. "Bryce became the surfer he is through good old-fashioned hard work. He's the best, plain and simple."

I smiled and said, "It seems the judges think so. Do they have the same judges at every competition?"

"Not usually, though there is one who seems to show up at most of the competitions that Bryce does. He's the head judge today, so he must be quite renowned. Probably judges all of the surfing competitions."

That could be.

If he was the head judge, he could have more sway with how things were scored. I didn't know how these things worked or how much power the head judge actually had, but it sounded like an impressive title.

Unfortunately, I couldn't ask Felicity outright if she thought Bryce was paying off the head judge and keeping Isaac from the win that I felt he deserved, so I instead introduced her to Dottie and Jessie and offered her a granola bar.

It wasn't more than two minutes later that it was announced the first heat of the day would begin shortly. Apparently, only four surfers would be out on the waves at the same time, battling it out for the best score.

And just our luck, Isaac and Bryce were both in the first heat.

Judging by their earlier threats, assigning them to surf at the same time seemed like a dangerous choice.

I HADN'T KNOWN what to expect at a surfing competition. There were rules I didn't understand, and the more it was explained to me, the more confused I became.

Apparently, the rounds were divided into heats where the surfers' best two waves would be averaged together. This heat would last around twenty-five minutes. That seemed like a long time to me, especially when there were four men out there who had something to prove.

People around me were throwing around unfamiliar

terms, like who had priority. It sounded like it was a way to take turns so the surfers didn't purposely steal someone else's wave. Jessie was shouting, saying Bryce had interfered with Isaac, while Felicity insisted he'd done nothing of the sort.

None of it made sense to me, and I focused on whether Isaac had stayed on his board.

We were near the end of the first heat when Jessie sucked in a hard breath.

"What?" Dottie asked, just as confused as I was. "Did something happen?"

"Isaac got to the lineup first so he has priority, but see how Bryce is positioning himself? I think he's going to try to go for that wave. He'll be penalized if he does."

We watched anxiously as Isaac stood up on his board. He rode the wave like the pro he was, even popping up over the top of the wave and getting air before coming back down, like it hadn't taken any effort at all.

But then Bryce showed up out of nowhere, cutting Isaac off, causing our lifeguard to tumble off his surfboard. As he did so, though, Isaac flung himself toward Bryce, both of them disappearing under the wave.

Their boards popped up, and so did Isaac, his movements frantic. Even from this distance, I could sense that something was seriously wrong.

Because even though Bryce's board had resurfaced, the surfer hadn't.

3

Felicity paced in front of us, raking her fingers through her hair. "He shouldn't be down there that long. Even if he got ragdolled, he'd have resurfaced by now."

"I wouldn't worry," I said, though even I didn't believe me. "Isaac has been Starlight Ridge's lifeguard for years. Bryce is in good hands." Isaac had untethered himself from his surfboard and was now diving beneath the surface, presumably to look for Bryce.

Felicity spun toward me. "Are you kidding? Isaac is the reason Bryce is in this situation in the first place. He purposely knocked Bryce into the water."

"To be fair," Jessie said, "if Bryce hadn't interfered with Isaac's wave—"

"Honest mistake," Felicity said, cutting her off. "It's not

always easy to see everyone's position when you're out there. Bryce would never purposely do that."

So, even she was admitting that Bryce had interfered. Whatever his motives, the mistake had been to put him and Isaac out there together. I was surprised something like this hadn't happened sooner.

"And Isaac would never allow someone to drown. Not on his watch," Jessie said.

I could tell that neither Felicity nor Jessie thought much of the other, and I stepped between them. "The important thing is that—"

"Isaac is pulling him out of the water," Felicity interrupted.

"Yes, that Isaac can help Bryce is the most important thing," Jessie agreed.

Felicity shook her head and pointed. "No, Isaac is pulling Bryce out of the water," she repeated, then she sprinted toward the beach, where Isaac was struggling under Bryce's weight.

Before Felicity had reached the shoreline, medics had already helped Isaac lift Bryce farther onto the sand. One of them immediately started CPR.

Felicity paced back and forth like a caged animal, throwing anxious glances at the gathering crowd.

It had only been a few minutes, though it felt like an eternity, when the medic's hands stilled, no longer giving compressions. His forehead glistened with sweat, and he pushed back a lock of hair from his eyes. His gaze found Felicity's, then dropped.

I couldn't hear the words exchanged, but I got the gist of it when Felicity fell to her knees, sobbing.

Bryce Carlton was dead.

I SHOULDN'T HAVE BEEN SURPRISED by the immediate response from law enforcement. Extra security had been hired, due to the large number of visitors, most of them coming in from the big city forty-five minutes away. They were likely off-duty police officers looking to earn some extra money on the side, and they'd now established a perimeter, keeping even Felicity away from the body.

It wasn't these big-city police officers who were in charge, though.

They were taking orders from a man who wore a baseball cap and board shorts. His Hawaiian shirt was covered in palm trees, and yet no one questioned what he asked of them.

"Sheriff Hart," I called, waving my arms wildly. I hadn't seen the man in several months—not since he'd attempted to escort me to prison. Even though I hadn't loved being arrested for murder, I still held a fondness for the man. He was stationed in a town thirty minutes up the coast, however, and he only visited when necessary.

The sheriff couldn't hear me, so I squeezed myself through the crowd until I reached the police tape.

"My sister and I are consultants for the sheriff," I told one of the security officers when he crossed his arms over his chest. I pointed to Sheriff Hart, who had taken off his baseball cap and was running his fingers through his hair.

The security officer raised an eyebrow as he glanced over his shoulder at our small-town sheriff. He turned back. "He hires old women to help him with his cases?" He sounded skeptical.

Consultant was maybe the wrong term. We'd helped him solve his last case, yes, but it had been more out of self-preservation than anything. And against his will. That being said, we did have skills that could prove helpful.

"My sister," I said, turning to where Dottie ought to be. I'd sworn she'd followed me, but instead I was met with a tourist who looked like he'd forgotten his sunscreen—his skin had turned a blinding shade of red. We made eye contact, and I smiled. "You're going to want some aloe vera for that, my dear. Drink plenty of water, get some rest, and you might be okay by the end of the week."

The man did not look like he appreciated my advice.

I gave him one last smile to make sure he knew I only meant to help, then turned my attention to finding Dottie. She was right back where we'd been sitting, and she was munching on some sort of churro. Since when did Starlight Ridge sell those?

I spotted the food trucks lining the boardwalk.

That figured. Rather than allowing people the opportunity to enjoy the local cuisine, the event organizers were treating the event as a traveling carnival. And Dottie was encouraging it.

"My sister," I started again, turning back to the large security officer. He looked like he was less police officer and more Navy SEAL. "She's a retired police officer and has plenty of expertise in these types of things. Sheriff Hart is lucky to have us."

The officer's gaze bore into me as he studied me. "Sheriff Hart," he barked over his shoulder, startling me. "This woman says she works for you."

I held up a finger. "I never said that—"

I stopped mid-sentence. The officer wasn't listening to me, instead chuckling at the surprise etched in the sheriff's face as he walked over.

"Jo, you don't work for me. I appreciate you as a friend. I appreciate your pastries. But I do not appreciate your investigative tendencies."

I cocked an eyebrow. "You nearly sent me to prison for the rest of my life, Sheriff—imagine living with that kind of guilt. It's because of my investigative tendencies that you discovered the truth, and I feel that deserves at least some appreciation. Dottie and I can help—you know we can."

Sheriff Hart gave a quick shake of his head. "No. I have enough help, thank you. More than enough."

"But it wasn't Isaac's fault," I insisted, even as he turned away. "And Dottie and I can prove it."

That gave him pause. The sheriff turned back slowly. "What do you know, Jo?"

I hadn't gotten that far, and I tried to think fast. There had to be something, but the only encounters I'd had with Bryce had been when he and Isaac had been fighting, and then when I'd insulted Bryce. And then again when I'd tried to make amends and he'd ignored me. None of that was useful in the moment.

Sheriff Hart sighed. "Yes, that's what I thought." He paused. "Jo, I'm very busy. Please stay out of things and let us do our jobs." And then he walked away.

"It sounds like your consulting won't be needed after all," the large security officer said with an annoying smirk.

I spun away. Fine. I'd let the sheriff do his job. But if he dared even insinuate that Isaac had killed Bryce, I couldn't guarantee that I'd stay out of things.

"How'd it go?" Dottie asked when I rejoined her and Jessie.

I sat down with a heavy thud. "You know the sheriff. He's stubborn and won't admit that he likes having us around."

Dottie smiled, and her gaze settled on the ocean.

I knew we should probably return to the bakery. With all these tourists and no surfing event, they'd likely be wandering the town for the rest of the day. Once we flipped the OPEN sign, we'd sell out of our pastries within the hour.

I just couldn't bring myself to do it, though.

So I followed Dottie's lead, allowing my attention to turn to the ocean. We sat in comfortable silence, the chaos around us fading until it was barely noticeable. I'd lived in New Mexico for the past two decades, and all this water—it had been a bit of a shock when I'd moved to Starlight Ridge. I still wasn't used to it. I could stare at the ocean for hours, and it never got old.

I closed my eyes, relishing the feel of the sun on my face, the sound of the ocean waves crashing against the shore in the background.

So beautiful. Yet so deadly.

Maybe that was why I liked it so much.

"Jo," Dottie said, touching my sleeve.

I started. When I opened my eyes, I realized the sun was in a different position, and the chaos that had surrounded us had disappeared. There was no one left. How long had I been sitting there? I had a feeling I was going to have a sunburn as severe as the tourist I'd met earlier. Good thing I was stocked up on aloe vera.

"We should get going," Dottie said, standing and stretching. "An ambulance took Bryce a while ago, and the news vans are busy chasing different angles of the story."

I used the arms of the folding chair for balance as I worked to push myself up. Sometime while I'd been sleeping, my muscles had stopped working, and my back acted like it wasn't meant to straighten.

Jessie was no longer sitting with us, both her and her chair gone. My sister noticed where my gaze had landed, and she added, "Jessie said to leave the chairs and she'll come back to collect them later."

"We can return the chairs—she shouldn't have to do all of the work, cleaning up after us," I said stubbornly, finally getting to my feet.

Dottie raised an eyebrow. "You're going to carry your chair all the way back to Jessie's place?"

I wanted to. I'd been trying to get strong. There was the yoga class on Tuesdays and Thursdays, parkour on Fridays, and I'd even begun to do some strength training. The longer I could keep this body of mine going, the better.

But no, I wouldn't be carrying my chair to Jessie's place. It was probably a quarter of a mile, and I hated myself for not being able to do even that much.

I frowned, and Dottie rested a hand on my shoulder. She smiled kindly. "It's okay. We are doing the best we can with what we've got. There's no shame in that."

"I know," I said. As if I believed her.

As I picked up my beach bag, Dottie's gaze landed somewhere beyond my shoulder, and she nodded. "Is that Felicity?"

I turned and noticed a figure with pink-streaked hair standing close enough to the ocean that the water lapped over her feet. She was alone.

"It is," I said. "We should see if she needs anything."

Even though we had been rooting for opposing competitors, I didn't like that none of her friends had stuck around to comfort her. All those people who had surrounded Bryce earlier, they'd disappeared just as quickly as he had. From all appearances, she had no one.

Dottie and I approached her, our steps cautious.

"Felicity?" I said, my words soft. "Would you like us to walk with you back to your hotel? Food and rest do wonders for the soul."

She didn't turn from the ocean, a light breeze playing with her hair. "There's nothing that calms me more than the ocean. Even though..." Her voice hitched. "Even though it's what took Bryce from me. Its power is incredible, isn't it? It provides life for entire species, but it can take life just as easily."

"Nature is both beautiful and terrifying," I agreed.

Felicity turned to face us. "People are the same way. Both beautiful and terrible."

I felt I knew where she might be taking this line of conversation, and I wasn't interested in it. Only wanted to make sure that Felicity was okay.

"Is there anything we can do for you?" Dottie asked, also seeming to sense what Felicity was implying, and moving the conversation in a different direction. I was grateful to her for it. "We need to get back to the bakery—Autumn is likely trying to run it singlehandedly, even though we told her to go home and get some rest. She's our baker, and she'll work herself into the ground if we don't intervene."

Felicity turned back to the ocean. "No. Thank you." A pause. "As much as you don't want to admit it, Bryce's death—it's Isaac's fault. Whether intentional or not, I've already received assurances from police that they'll pursue a criminal investigation."

So much for moving the conversation in another direction.

"It was an accident," I said. "You know that—you must. Surfing is an inherently dangerous sport, and while I agree that both men had a part to play in the events that transpired today, it was still just that. An accident."

Felicity spun toward us, and both Dottie and I took an instinctive step backwards.

"It was no accident, and I will ensure that your sheriff, every news agency, and every social media influencer knows it."

And then Felicity stalked away, sand spraying as she went.

"How do you feel that went?" Dottie said as we turned toward the boardwalk. She shot me a look of amusement so I'd know she was kidding—that it was obvious how that had gone.

"I'm inclined to say badly," I said with a hint of a smile. "And I think Isaac may need some support. You don't think the town will blame him for what happened, do you? He needs to know he can at least count on Starlight Ridge until the fallout from this tragedy blows over. If Felicity has it her way, Isaac will be on the black list of every surfing organization in the world."

Dottie gave a sad shake of her head. "No, Felicity

doesn't just want him blacklisted. She wants his name to be synonymous with Bryce's death forever, his reputation destroyed. For her, that includes prison."

I scoffed. "I'm sure this isn't the first time someone has knocked another surfer off their board. Surely the sheriff, and the surfing community, will understand that."

We stepped onto the boardwalk and turned right. When we rounded the corner, we saw that Autumn had indeed opened the bakery and a line already snaked out the door.

"I wouldn't bet on it," Dottie said. "Those people who are so eager to buy our pastries right now could very well be the same people who will destroy Isaac in the coming days, and Starlight Ridge along with it."

Oy vey.

4

D ottie flipped the CLOSED sign in our bakery's front window. "What a day," she said. "It started with us thinking our bakery was burning down, made a smooth transition to Bryce's murder, and then ended with us on our feet for eight hours until we literally had no more pastries to sell. Even with Autumn baking at record speeds back there. I guess grieving people need to soothe their pain somehow."

She looked at where I lay on the bakery's cold tile floor and raised an eyebrow. "How do you think you're going to get up from there? I don't have the energy to get myself up the stairs to our apartment, let alone lift you off the floor."

I shifted my head, trying to see her. My back had been so tight and achy that as soon as Dottie had locked the front door, I'd collapsed right where I'd been standing. The floor was dirty and disgusting, and I had no idea how I was going to get back up, but at least my pain had diminished.

"Autumn will help me."

Our pâtissiere entered at that moment, looking like she was nearer to death than I was. "I'll do my best, but I'm so exhausted, I can barely think straight. I can't believe how inconsiderate our customers were, and yet it was in a 'don't worry, be happy' kind of way. Like they had no regard for anyone but themselves, and they wanted us to take it with a smile." She collapsed onto a stool behind the checkout counter. "Remember that family who wanted macarons after we'd sold out? They asked how long it would take to make more, and when they didn't like the answer, they pushed until I agreed to a timetable that shouldn't have been possible. And they wanted a discount for the inconvenience of having to return."

"Not all surfing folk are like that, though," Dottie said, joining Autumn behind the counter.

Autumn conceded. "You're right. Most of the people who came into the bakery today were lovely, and I'm letting a few bad apples make me grumpy. I'm just tired."

"And understandably so," I said from the floor. "You need to go home, like I've been trying to get you to do all day. I wouldn't have minded kicking that family out and telling them that if the macarons were so important to them, they could buy them elsewhere."

Autumn gave me a weak smile. "There isn't anywhere else in town they could have purchased macarons."

"That would have been their problem, not ours," I said. It looked like I had reached my grumpy phase as well.

Dottie chuckled. "Well, lesson learned. Next time we have a big event like this, we establish rules for ourselves that we refuse to break. Our sanity is worth more than random strangers getting their éclairs or napoleons."

From where I was lying on the floor, I couldn't see Dottie or Autumn, so I used my feet to spin me in a circle so I was facing them. I was going to need a really long shower after I made it upstairs. I tried not to think about what I was currently covered in. Sand, for sure. Dirt, absolutely. Seagull dung that someone had tracked in on their shoes...probably.

"How's your back feeling?" Dottie asked with a smirk.

"Peachy," I said. At least it felt better than when I had been standing. "We shouldn't wait to make those rules, though. Even though the competition has been canceled, I think we should have them in place for those attendees who decide to stay for the remainder of the week."

"Agreed," Autumn said, her words muffled. She was now bent over the counter, her head nestled in her arms, like she was going to sleep there for the night.

"Rule one," Dottie said. "We stay closed tomorrow. I don't care how much money these people wave at us; we need a day to recuperate. And Autumn needs to sleep."

Autumn raised her head and looked like she might protest, but resigned to laying her head back down. "Agreed."

A knock on the bakery's door made me jump, and I used my feet to spin my body so I could see who was crazy enough to think we'd sell them pastries at eight o'clock at night. What time did these tourists plan on staying out until?

But it wasn't a tourist.

It was Sheriff Hart.

I groaned. "If he thinks our pastries killed this guy too, I'm going to give him a piece of my mind. I cannot be put in handcuffs again. I still have nightmares that I'm sitting in a jail cell."

"The only jail cell you stayed in had a deputy waiting on you hand and foot," Dottie said. I could practically hear the eye roll as she pushed herself up from the stool.

I raised a finger, my gaze on the ceiling as I waited for Dottie to come into my line of sight. "I was nearly taken to the real prison—the one that doesn't appreciate what a wonderful person I am. And that was enough to scare me straight."

Another knock on the door. Sheriff Hart wore a frown that told me this wasn't a social visit and he wasn't feeling very patient.

"I'm coming," Dottie grumbled. She leaned on her cane more than usual, her footsteps shuffling forward as she unlocked the front door. "This better be good," she told the sheriff, gesturing for him to enter. "We're barely holding it together in here." She nodded at me. "Case in point."

Sheriff Hart looked down at me but didn't look the least bit surprised to find me lying on the floor. As if sensing we had visitors, Skittles decided this would be a good time to wander into the shop from wherever she'd been hiding. She walked around my prone body, sniffed a couple of times, then stepped right on top of me, ultimately curling up in a furry pile on my stomach.

"Oh, come on," I said. "Now how am I going to get up?"

Dottie snorted. "Yeah, like you would have been able to even before Skittles settled in for the night."

That earned at least a glimmer of a smile from Sheriff Hart, and he extended a hand toward me. "May I?"

I hated to make Skittles move after she'd just gotten comfortable. But at the same time, this floor was getting colder, and I swore, dirtier, by the second.

"Yes, thank you," I said, reaching for the sheriff's hand.

Skittles gave an annoyed meow but leaped off and found a stool to settle on instead.

It took Sheriff Hart more than just a helping hand to get me off the floor, though. I didn't have the strength to pull myself up, and he ended up having to get behind me to push me into a sitting position. He then crouched down so I could use his shoulder while he straightened into a standing position. Ten minutes later, I was on my feet. Filthy and embarrassed at what it had taken to get me standing again, but at least I wouldn't be sleeping on the floor tonight.

"You came at just the right time," I told the sheriff.

"How did you know what kind of predicament I'd gotten myself into? Maybe you have Beatrice's gift."

Beatrice had been my and Dottie's eldest sister—the one who'd turned this gorgeous bakery into a tacky souvenir shop where she'd sold clearance items and tarot cards. At least she'd been happy. Paranoid and completely bonkers, of course, but happy. She'd also had a connection with the universe the rest of us didn't. A third eye, if you will. Neither Dottie nor I had been blessed with that gift.

This time Sheriff Hart really did smile. A genuine one. "I don't have the gift of intuition and foresight like your sister, but I do have an inclination toward investigation."

I jutted out my chin and stuck my hands on my hips. "I didn't do it, and you know it. I have no connection to Bryce Carlton, other than accidentally insulting him right before the competition." I paused when the sheriff raised an eyebrow. "Fine, I will admit that part wasn't accidental, but I wouldn't kill him just so Isaac could win. Besides, how would I? It's not like I know my way around a surfboard—"

The sheriff held up a hand. "I don't think you killed Bryce," he said. "But your guilty conscience now has me wondering if you know more than you're saying."

I clamped my lips shut and silently shook my head.

Sheriff Hart's gaze turned to Dottie. "Unlike your sister, I know you'd never purposely impede an investigation. You have anything for me?"

Dottie held his gaze. "No, sorry. You know I would help if I could, especially if it would take the heat off of Isaac.

It's no secret there was bad blood between the two surfers, but from the way I hear it, bad blood seemed to be the norm for Bryce Carlton. There were allegations of him cheating in competitions, you know."

Sheriff Hart nodded slowly. "Yes, I had heard that." He paused and then looked at me, his expression guilty. "I don't think you had anything to do with Bryce's death, but I do need to ask you about the pastry you gave Bryce just before he competed."

I stared. How did he know about that? Oh, right. All the reporters and their cameras.

Dottie snorted. "You've got to be kidding me. This again? What is with people thinking we're the old ladies from *Arsenic and Old Lace*, determined to poison everyone?"

"Don't shoot the messenger," Sheriff Hart said, lifting his hands in a defensive gesture. "The thing is, other than some bruises and a couple lacerations, Bryce Carlton wasn't injured when he was knocked off his board. His friends said he was looking pale before the competition started, but he insisted he was fine. They didn't believe him."

"You really are thinking it was poison," I said, finding my voice.

The sheriff looked at me, his gaze studious. "Yes. We're still waiting on the toxicology report, but his lungs were filled with air. Not water."

My breath caught in my throat. "How is that possible?

He wasn't dead before he fell into the ocean. We all saw him surfing until Isaac leaped at him." I realized a moment too late how that sounded. "Not that Isaac is responsible for Bryce's death. I suppose he just thought it fair that if Bryce was going to knock him off balance, he'd return the favor."

Sheriff Hart ran a hand through his hair, and he blew out a hard breath. "That's the thing. Isaac said he wasn't trying to knock him into the water. He was trying to catch him."

5

Autumn had stayed quiet, her head resting on the counter, likely trying to stay as inconspicuous as possible. She suffered from intense anxiety, and she still didn't trust the sheriff after he'd suspected both Autumn and me of murder several months earlier.

She was alert now, though, her head popping up. "Come again?" she said.

The sheriff started, like he hadn't even realized she was there. He smoothed his uniform with his hands in an attempt to cover the sudden movement.

"Isaac says he was trying to save Bryce's life before he'd even fallen from his surfboard," the sheriff repeated. "Apparently, Bryce had been looking shaky when he cut Isaac off, as if he hadn't meant to, and then he doubled over in pain. Isaac claims he was trying to save Bryce's life." He paused. "I looked at the raw camera footage from the event, and it could be true, but it's difficult to tell from the angles the cameras were positioned at."

Pride swelled in my chest for our local lifeguard. Isaac was the type of person who would do everything he could to save the life of a rival, and I was grateful that Starlight Ridge could claim him as our own.

"Then why are you treating this as a murder?" I asked. "Maybe Bryce had health problems that he'd been keeping under wraps. Maybe he shouldn't have been out there in the first place."

"I wish it were that simple," Sheriff Hart said, leaning against the counter. He looked tired, like it had been the longest day of his life and all he wanted was to be home in bed. I could sympathize with the feeling. "The athletes needed a full physical checkup before being allowed to participate in the competition. A doctor had to sign off on it and everything. Bryce Carlton was the epitome of physical health when he showed up this morning."

That was a problem.

"Does that mean you've arrested Isaac?" Autumn asked, her voice small.

Sheriff Hart hesitated. "I don't know if arrested is the right word."

"Do you have him locked up?" Dottie asked, her tone holding impatience.

The sheriff didn't seem to want to answer that question either. "Technically, yes."

"So, you've arrested him and hauled him off to your jail

in Brighton's Beach?" I asked. I hoped Deputy Randy took as good care of Isaac as he had me.

"No, not at all. He's still here in Starlight Ridge, where he belongs." The sheriff's voice was firm—this was finally an answer he could be confident in. "Several months ago, when I was starting to spend a lot of time here in Starlight Ridge...too much time...I cleaned up the old sheriff's office you have here. Cleared out the garbage and dead rats, replaced the computers, got the electricity going—all that kind of stuff. I even have a proper office—nearly. Right now, it's only a desk, but it's a nice solid piece of furniture. Deputy Randy is keeping an eye on Isaac tonight and making sure no angry fans make their way inside."

"Oh, is he?" I asked, brightening. "I'm quite fond of Randy. He was a real sweetheart when you arrested me. A proper gentleman."

Sheriff Hart chuckled and shook his head. "Yes, a little too much of one, if you ask me. Can't go around giving room service to all our murder suspects."

I waved a hand through the air. "He knew I hadn't done it."

Autumn raised her hand. "Sorry to interrupt, but can we revisit the fact that you have Isaac locked up in a cell, but you haven't arrested him? I'm a little fuzzy on how that is legal."

Dottie gave a firm nod. "Yes, I'd like to hear more on that as well. Because, to answer Autumn's question, that's not legal, strictly speaking. At least it wasn't legal twenty years ago when I was still a cop, and I'm pretty sure not much has changed since then. It's different than sticking someone in the drunk tank overnight to let them sleep it off."

The sheriff looked uncomfortable under our gazes, and he pushed off from the counter, taking a step back. "Okay, I did arrest him. But I had to. Honestly, it's more for his protection than anything else."

Dottie snorted. "Is that how you sleep at night? By telling yourself those lies?"

Sheriff Hart stilled, and his gaze settled on each of us. "Whatever your feelings about Bryce Carlton, you have a town filled with his fans. And they think that Isaac killed him."

I hadn't thought of it like that. Isaac was well known in the circuit, but he hadn't competed recently. He was old news. A local hero that no one else seemed to be rooting for anymore.

These people would want justice.

"Is that the only reason you arrested him?" Dottie asked, her voice quiet. "For protection?"

Sheriff Hart hesitated. "No. He's also the only person with motive, and opportunity."

"Isaac trying to catch Bryce when he fell off his surfboard isn't opportunity," I said. "You need to be looking at who had the opportunity to poison him. Who surrounded him in his downtime and who had access to his water or food. The person who is the answer to that question—it isn't Isaac."

"I know." The sheriff's gaze turned to me. "Tell me more about this bread pudding you made for Bryce."

Dottie, Autumn, and I stared, incredulous, then all three of us started talking at once.

"We are not doing this again," Dottie said.

Autumn jutted out her chin. "You're not taking her."

"If you think—" I started, giving the sheriff the best stink eye I could muster, but then I paused and looked at Dottie and Autumn. "Wait, why do you automatically assume he suspects me when asking about the bread pudding? Why not either of you two? You had equal access to it."

Sheriff Hart had to have known what would happen when he mentioned the bread pudding, so I didn't know why he looked so surprised at our outbursts.

"That's not what I'm saying," he shouted, attempting to be heard above all the noise.

Dottie eyed him warily. "So, what is it that you are saying, dear sheriff?"

He released a long breath. "I don't know yet what the poison was or how it was administered. I don't even know for sure that poison was involved. Maybe he had an allergic reaction to something he ate. There is no evidence that your bread pudding had anything to do with it. But if it was an allergy, I do need to know everything that was in your pastry."

When we still didn't look convinced, he slumped onto one of the stools at the display counter. "I'm just trying to cover all my bases while I'm waiting to hear back from the hospital. Honest. I can ask people to stick around town while I conduct my investigation, but that doesn't mean they're going to, which means I need to move quickly. The judges and coaches haven't exactly been easy to work with."

"I forgot about them," I said, then walked into the back kitchen, where I knew Autumn kept a small whiteboard to write ideas for new variations on her recipes. When I returned with it, Autumn was listing off the ingredients for her bread pudding for the sheriff.

"You're wasting your time. Bryce didn't even eat it. His girlfriend did," I said.

They didn't pay me any attention, so I sat at the counter and wrote SUSPECTS on the top of the board. I then wrote HEAD JUDGE under it, because I didn't know his name. Under that, I wrote COACH. The judge likely wouldn't have had easy access to Bryce's food, but the coach would have. Maybe the judge had worked with someone else.

I looked at my list thus far. Only two people. That wasn't much, and I wasn't about to add Isaac's name to the list. So, who else would have had the opportunity?

As soon as I asked the question, I pictured the group of people surrounding Bryce. His entourage. All the cameras.

Sheriff Hart finally noticed me and walked over. "What do you have there?"

"I thought I'd start writing down everyone who might have had an opportunity to get close to Bryce. Trust me when I say that the people of Starlight Ridge will stand behind Isaac every step of the way, and that means proving he couldn't have had anything to do with Bryce's murder." I glanced at the sheriff. "Don't worry, I know he's safest in your jail cell—for the time being. That's why this is the best way we can help him."

Dottie walked up and glanced at the board. "You haven't got much on there, do you?"

I released a sigh. "And even this is useless. When I stopped by to visit Bryce and give him the bread pudding, he was waxing his surfboard. Didn't look at me—refused to talk to me. He was in what his girlfriend called 'the zone.' She said he wouldn't eat unless she reminded him."

The sheriff perked up at that. "So, you're saying the girlfriend could have done it."

I picked up the dry erase marker, but even as I wrote FELICITY on the board, I said, "The reason I said this list is useless is because he was surrounded by people. There had to be at least seven people hanging around him at the time, and that's not including reporters and camera people. There are countless people who could have wished him harm—he wasn't exactly known for his people skills. And let's not forget the people who thought he was cheating but couldn't prove how."

Sheriff Hart studied the board, his gaze intense, though there were only the three names on it. His phone rang, shattering the silence that had settled over us, but it took him a minute to register that the call was intended for him.

"I should get this," he said, slipping out his phone and glancing at the screen. "It's the hospital." He looked at us. "Thank you for your input, but I'll take it from here. And when I say that, I mean please do yourselves, and me, a favor and erase the names on your board."

And then he half-ran out the bakery's front doors as he answered a call that I desperately wished I could eavesdrop on.

"He's right," Dottie said. "This is his job. He's the one who has access to the test results, as well as all of the video footage."

"And yet he's locked Isaac up," I muttered, still grumpy about it, even though I knew it was for the best.

"I would have done the same thing. I believe him when he says that Isaac is safer in that jail cell than out here with all the crazies." Dottie pushed herself off the stool she sat on, grimacing as she did so. "Jo, if I'm not out of bed before you in the morning, come and check on me. It is very possible that I'll be stuck."

I gave a distracted nod. "Sure. No problem. Stuck."

When I realized that both Dottie and Autumn were looking at me funny, their eyebrows raised in concern, I gave them a smile. "Don't look at me like that. We're letting the sheriff and his deputy do their jobs, and we are finally going to bed and getting the rest we deserve. All is right in the world."

And then I said goodnight and turned toward the stairs.

"Autumn, we were serious when we said not to come in tomorrow," I called over my shoulder. "You need a day off, as do we. We'll still pay you, of course." I knew that Autumn relied on this job and, although a day off was nice, a paid day off was better. Especially considering how hard she'd been working for the surfing event.

"Are you sure?" Autumn asked, looking between the two of us. "I know we're not normally open on Sundays, but people are still here for the competition and have nothing to do but wander around town and eat. If today is any indication, it will be a big business day for us."

I glanced at Dottie to gauge her reaction. She was studying me, not like she was annoyed but more like she thought I was up to something.

But then she smiled and turned to Autumn. "Of course. We won't have a bakery if we work you, and ourselves, so hard that we kill ourselves in the process. And I don't just mean that figuratively." She looked at me. "You really do need to check on me in the morning."

I smiled. "I know. And I will."

And then I started up the stairs, because I didn't want my sister to see the truth I was trying to hide from her.

That she was right. I was up to something.

The cat could tell, though. Skittles gracefully leaped

from the stool she'd curled up on and darted up the stairs. When she reached the top of the staircase, she turned to look down at me, accusation in her eyes.

"There's nothing wrong with helping a friend," I told her.

She stared at me a moment longer before retreating to Dottie's bedroom.

Good thing she couldn't tell on me.

6

I had big plans for our day off.

Autumn called early to say that church, and bingo, were canceled because of the ongoing murder investigation. I acted disappointed. Anyone who knew me knew that I never allowed anything to come between me and my bingo. Church was just the vehicle to get there. Our pastor had reinstated what he was now calling the 'Salvation Bingo Card': if you came to church, you got an extra card. It looked prettier than the others, so people knew you'd been to church—a light blue background, clouds, and Jesus descending from the top.

Others in town thought it was inappropriate, but I didn't think Jesus would mind. In fact, I wouldn't be surprised if Jesus himself was a bingo fan. Besides, it wasn't like we were gambling. We didn't pay money to play bingo, and the prizes were donated. This made it extra exciting, because you never knew what you would get. Last month I had won a Monkees album, on vinyl. I no longer had a record player, but it had still been fun to win it.

Today, though—today I had other places I needed to be.

The sheriff had said he didn't need my help, and it was true that he had access to information that I didn't. But he was also a sheriff, which meant that people clammed up whenever he was around. Right now, Isaac might be in a jail cell because it was the safest place for him, but if Sheriff Hart didn't get any other leads, it would be Isaac's word against hundreds of eyewitnesses that he had been trying to save Bryce, not kill him.

I thought I knew whose word a jury would believe.

Whether the sheriff would admit it or not, we had helped him in the past, and we could help him again.

"I'm glad we decided to stay closed today," Dottie called from her bedroom. When I had checked on her, she had indeed been stuck in bed, and it had taken a day's worth of energy just to pull her onto her feet.

"Yes, it will be nice to relax and see where the day takes us," I called back as I dressed in my own bedroom.

A pause.

"What are you up to, Jo?"

I thought it had been a generic thing to say and had no idea what part of it had tipped her off. I moved to pull on my blouse, but my arm got stuck in one of the sleeves. "Nothing. I only meant that without church and bingo, and with the store being closed, we have the whole day ahead of us."

My arm broke free, and I began buttoning the front. I listened for Dottie.

Silence.

I poked my head out into the hallway. "What are your plans for the day?"

It was another moment before Dottie exited her bedroom and moved toward the bathroom. "What did you say? I only caught the first part."

I noticed she hadn't put her hearing aids in yet. "I asked what your plans are for the day."

She pulled her aids out of their case. "Keeping you out of trouble."

I laughed. "What kind of trouble could I possibly get in?"

"Asks the woman who stole evidence in the last murder investigation and was nearly convicted herself," she said over her shoulder.

My heart dropped. So, that was what this was. As tired as Dottie was—and I could tell she needed to spend the day off her feet—she was worried that if she let me go out wandering on my own that I'd investigate. And I'd get myself into trouble.

"You mean you intend to babysit me today," I said, my voice quiet.

Dottie had been trying to protect me from my klepto-mania since we were children. When I'd moved away from our family home in Kansas to New Mexico to attend college, she hadn't thought it was wise for me to be on my own and had tried to talk me out of it. I had managed, though. Or at least managed to return everything before people noticed.

This last time, though...it had changed things. I supposed I had both expected, and deserved, that Dottie would be more cautious about me going places on my own now.

Dottie exited the bathroom, looking freshened up and ready for the day. Like I hadn't literally pulled her out of bed. "Look, most of the time, your...condition...isn't a big deal. At least, nothing we can't handle. But right now, with all these people here—you shouldn't be out there on your own." Her gaze met mine. "Especially when I know you are planning on interfering with the sheriff's investigation."

I frowned. "That's a harsh way of putting it. I don't interfere—I help."

Dottie massaged her eyebrows and bent her head. "You know how I feel about getting involved with active police investigations. When I was on the police force, if you had pulled any of your stunts that you have with Sheriff Hart—"

"You would have had me arrested," I finished for her. "Yes, you've told me this many times. Despite that, you also crossed that line to save your dear sister earlier this year. Which I thank you for, by the way."

Dottie raised her head, her gaze settling on me. "Why

won't you let me protect you? It's like you go out of your way to stir things up and test the limits. You're nearly seventy and yet you act like you're seventeen, with me still having to clean up after you." She paused. "When we decided to move to Starlight Ridge, I thought things would be different. We hadn't seen each other for years and hadn't lived with each other for decades. We were even opening a business together. But it's not different, and I'm just now realizing that it never will be."

The way Dottie was talking—this wasn't something new. She'd felt like this for a long time. Maybe for the entire year since we'd moved to Starlight Ridge. She regretted moving out here with me.

"I'm sorry you've had to carry the burden for so long," I said, hoping she caught the sarcasm. "Please, let me relieve you of it."

And then I left the apartment, refusing to look back at Dottie. Refusing to see if she cared that I was leaving. And more importantly, not giving her the time to follow me.

I used the back entrance of the apartment, exiting onto a small lane that wound behind the homes and shops on the boardwalk. I didn't know where I would go. The original plan had been to see if I could locate the panel of judges that Bryce had supposedly bribed. I doubted he could bribe an entire panel, but if he could get to one, that would be enough. I assumed it would have to be the head judge—the one who had been present at most of the competitions. He would be the most likely culprit.

And that had been the plan.

Now?

I wasn't in the mood.

My own sister—someone who I had considered a partner—saw me as a weight around her neck. Someone who was dragging her down. A nuisance she was constantly having to deal with.

I understood it, but that didn't mean I liked it. She was forgetting that before we had moved out here together, I had lived on my own, and for quite some time too.

I was just passing behind the scuba shop when I heard a voice that made me stop mid-step. It was a woman's voice, and it was low and intense. She was somewhere just ahead of me on the path and seemed to be moving closer, so I stepped into the small alleyway between the laundromat and the scuba shop.

"Of course I didn't do it. That would be crazy. He might have been an insufferable surfer, but he still brought in the majority of my income."

A pause.

"I just talked with the sheriff. Actually, it was more of an interrogation. It seems Bryce was poisoned. They found belladonna berries in his stomach."

Another pause.

"Victor, where would I find belladonna berries?"

My feet were starting to tire, and I shifted so I could lean against the scuba shop. I hadn't noticed the dog poo that had been the original tenant of the space I wished to occupy, and I stepped squarely in it.

"Oh, you've got to be kidding me," I groaned, forgetting I was supposed to be quiet. After my glorious exit from the bakery, I didn't want to have to immediately return, covered in dog feces, no less.

The speaker grew quiet, whispered that she had to go, and immediately ended her conversation.

So much for stealth.

A few seconds later, a woman emerged around the corner and discovered me trying to hold onto the wall with one hand while scraping the poo off my shoe with a piece of cardboard I'd found on the ground.

I didn't know who she'd thought she might find in this little alleyway, but her tense expression relaxed when she saw it was only me.

"I thought I'd take a shortcut," I said, still scraping at the bottom of my shoe. "Thought it might be nice to take a walk where I wouldn't be overrun by all the tourists, and then I went and stepped in probably the only pile of dog poo in all of Starlight Ridge."

The woman looked to be the athletic type, her dark hair pulled back into a ponytail. She wore athletic wear, but it seemed expensive. The type of stuff celebrities wore when they were trying to pretend they were down to earth, like the rest of us.

She smiled and stepped forward. "Here, let me help

you." She held out her hand, I was sure expecting me to hand her the piece of cardboard.

I hesitated. Even though I was curious as to who this woman was and I wanted to prolong this interaction, it didn't feel right allowing her to scrape feces off my shoe. "I don't think we know each other well enough for that," I said. "I think I've gotten most of it, anyway."

The woman's smile widened. "I should probably introduce myself, then. My name is Lindi Fierce, and I'm afraid I'm one of those tourists you've been avoiding."

"Nice to meet you Lindi. I'm Jo Darby," I said, returning her smile. I tapped my finger on the wall, trying to remember where I'd heard her name before. It was familiar, but I couldn't remember why. "Lindi Fierce. Do we have any mutual acquaintances?"

Her smiled dipped, and her expression was suddenly guarded. "I don't think so." She held out a hand again for the cardboard. "Please, I'd like to help. But once you get home, you'll most certainly want to use a toothbrush to get all of the grooves. Another option is to shuffle your feet through the sand down at the beach. It's coarse enough that it will likely do the trick."

I was still stuck on where I'd heard that name before.

"Lindi Fierce," I repeated quietly to myself. My gaze popped up. "You were Bryce Carlton's coach. Isaac has only wonderful things to say about you, though he was disappointed when you chose Bryce over him. I suppose you couldn't coach both of them—that would be a conflict of interest. But now that Bryce won't be surfing anymore, or doing much of anything else..."

My voice trailed off as I realized how inappropriate that had been. Once again, my mouth had run faster than my brain. Maybe Dottie had been right. Maybe I did need a babysitter.

"I'm sorry, I shouldn't have said that," I started, but Lindi cut me off.

"Isaac wasn't half as disappointed as I was. He is a great guy, and a very talented surfer. Anyone would be lucky to coach him. Who is he working with now?"

"No one, I don't think," I said, shifting my weight to the other foot. Even with the parkour classes I'd been taking, I still had a ways to go with my balance. "He mostly enjoys being on his own, from what I can tell. He's the first one out there surfing in the early mornings, and then he life-guards during the day. He says when it's just him and the ocean, everything feels exactly as it should be."

Lindi nodded slowly as she held out her hand once more. I relented, handing her the piece of cardboard. "Will you take your shoe off, please?" she said. "It will be just for a moment."

I leaned against the wall and then held onto Lindi's shoulder with one hand as I struggled to remove my shoe with the other. After nearly losing my balance twice, I handed it to her.

"That doesn't sound like the Isaac I knew way back when," she said as she scraped at the sole of the shoe. "He was fearless, always pushing himself, and in turn, forcing others to do the same, just to keep up with him."

"So...why did you choose Bryce over Isaac?" I asked.

Lindi didn't answer right away, and she was far more focused on my shoe than she needed to be. Once she'd gotten the majority of the dog poo scraped off, she helped me get the shoe back on my foot.

When she straightened, she looked me in the eye. "You can tell Isaac that choosing Bryce was a mistake. And I've been paying for it ever since."

7

I wanted to ask Lindi what she'd meant by that—that she'd been paying for her choice to coach Bryce—but she immediately clammed up, like she'd said too much. Thankfully, she was still kind enough to offer me her arm as we walked back out onto the hidden pathway.

"Thank you for your help," I told her when we reached the end of the path. It would lead to the boardwalk just past Adeline's chocolate shop, which was the perfect place for me to be right now. I could use something sweet.

Lindi gave me a kind smile, but it now held deep sadness. "Anytime. And remember what I said—shuffle up and down the beach a few times, and that shoe should be as good as new." She then gave a little wave and hurried off into the crowd perusing the boardwalk shops. For whatever reason, the majority of spectators hadn't hightailed it out of Starlight Ridge as I had expected. Instead, they seemed determined to stay even longer.

It probably had something to do with the news cameras and vans. Apparently, they thought there was still a story to be had, and they were likely right, at least until the sheriff could discover who our murderer was.

All these people—they wanted to be a part of the narrative. A narrative that had left one surfer dead and his archrival sitting in a jail cell.

I looked forward to when all this would be over and the most exciting thing about my day would be Lars having a buy one, get one free sale on the breakfast platters over at the diner. He usually did that when his eggs were nearing their expiration date. It had been a while since the last sale—maybe I'd get lucky this weekend.

Bracing myself, I stepped out from behind the board-walk shops and was immediately hit with a cacophony of noise. I had gotten used to tourist season, but this felt completely different. It was more chaotic. Aggressive. I didn't like it.

I pulled a piece of hard candy from my purse, unwrapped it, and popped it into my mouth.

I paused after sucking on it for a few seconds—I hadn't brought any candy with me. And this was one of those weird strawberry ones that everyone's grandmothers filled their candy dish with, even though I'd never actually seen them sold in the stores.

I must have taken it from Lindi's pocket when she was

walking with me. I didn't even remember doing it, and I hoped she had a few more on her. Nothing was worse than looking forward to eating a sugary treat that you'd been saving, but then finding it was gone when you finally went to pull it out.

At least it had only been a candy I'd taken. In the past, I'd stolen a lot worse.

As much as I appreciated Lindi's involuntary donation, it wasn't what I needed in that moment, and I made a beeline for the chocolate shop. There was no comparison, and after the morning I'd had, I needed some of Adeline's chile chocolate truffles.

Unfortunately for me, the line snaked out the door of her shop. I moved to join the end of it but then saw that the last person standing in line was none other than Felicity.

I had felt attacked enough for one morning, so I made a sharp turn before she could see me. Unfortunately, my peripheral vision wasn't all that great anymore, and I ran right into...

"Sheriff Hart. Lovely to see you," I said, grabbing his arm and steadying myself. "I'm not investigating, I promise. I thought I'd grab a box of Adeline's chocolates, but as you can see, it's a bit busy this morning."

The sheriff's eyes smiled, though his mouth remained pressed in a firm line. "If you're in the mood for something sweet, I hear there's a wonderful French bakery on the next street over. You should try there."

I knew he was trying to make a joke, but it only made me think of how things had ended with Dottie that morning. "I'll...keep that in mind," I said, attempting a playful tone. It fell flat.

"Everything okay?" the sheriff asked, his eyebrows knit in concern.

I started to nod but then shook my head. "Nothing is okay," I said, moisture springing to my eyes. "A man is dead, Isaac is in jail, and it turns out that Bryce really was poisoned. Berries, of all things. I hate when people use food as a weapon. It feels wrong. To weaponize something like that—" I pulled in a long breath. "Dottie and I had to close our bakery today because we're old and need to recover from how crazy it was yesterday. I don't like getting old. It takes the fun out of everything. And then we got into a fight, Dottie and I. Apparently, I'm a burden. I don't mean to be. But you know how difficult my...condition...can be. In fact, I stole something just a few minutes ago. It only proves that I can't be left to my own devices and that Dottie was right. I'm not going to go back and tell her that, of course. She'll never let me forget..."

Sheriff Hart nodded polite hellos to those who were watching us with curious gazes, and then lightly took my arm and steered me through the crowd.

"You can't admit to stealing things out on a crowded street," he murmured. He didn't stop walking until we'd stepped around the corner and into our town's newly renovated sheriff's office.

As soon as we entered, I forgot what we'd even been talking about.

"This is beautiful," I told Sheriff Hart, turning in a circle. The last time I'd been in there, rotting garbage had been strewn everywhere, rats had made themselves at home, and the computers had been nothing more than outdated, and heavy, paperweights.

"We've done some good things in here," he said, seemingly trying to fight a smile. I didn't understand why he didn't allow his emotions to take center stage. He should be really proud of what he'd done with this space.

"I'm serious," I said, taking in the new desks and fancy computers. "It's unrecognizable. If I were arrested, I'd be honored to spend time in a jail like this."

The sheriff didn't seem to know how to take that, so he merely smiled and remained quiet.

"I consider myself honored, then," a voice said from the far end of the room. The holding cell.

"Isaac," I shouted, clapping my hands together. I walked as quickly as my feet would allow—which I could admit wasn't as fast as they usually did—and stopped just short of the bars.

Isaac stood against the back of the cell, leaning against the wall. Other than looking terribly tired, he looked all right.

"How is the sheriff treating you?" I peered through the bars to see what kind of bed they had given him. It was a twin bed on a metal frame. "I know the sleeping arrangements aren't ideal, but when I was arrested, they had the audacity to give me nothing but an old cot. That was never going to work for my bad back, of course, and Randy helped me get a bit of an upgrade. It seems they took my words to heart and got you a proper bed, so that's something."

Isaac pushed off from the wall and walked over to me. "Yes, the bed is fine, and they've been feeding me. I suppose that's all that can be expected, isn't it?"

"I could run home and grab Rummikub. Have you played that game? It's loads of fun and would help you pass the time in here. It's better with more players, so maybe we could get Randy to join us." I turned and searched the space for the sheriff's deputy. "He wasn't fired, I hope."

Sheriff Hart walked over. "No, he wasn't fired. Just running a couple of errands."

I looked at the sheriff, my lips parted in shock. "You left Isaac here all by himself? You said he was here for his own protection. And yet, I don't see any protection at all."

The sheriff rubbed his eyebrows, his head bowed, like it was taking all of his self-control to keep his patience with me. That seemed to be happening a lot today.

Isaac stepped in, rescuing the sheriff from needing to answer. "I'm fine, Jo. Really, I am. The only people I really need protection from are all those vulturous reporters, and the sheriff's done a good job of keeping them away."

"I don't doubt that the vultures are circling," I said.

"The more of your story I hear, the crazier it gets. Sheriff Hart says you were trying to rescue Bryce, even with the way he had treated you. I always knew you were one of the good ones, but that goes above and beyond. Seriously, they're going to make a movie about this someday. And you'll be the hero in it." I paused. "It might be one of those made-for-TV movies, but it will be just as good as the ones in the theater."

Isaac laughed, though his eyes were sad. "I hope they can find an actor who is as chiseled and handsome as I am. They're hard to come by."

I gave a solemn nod. "Isn't that the truth."

The sheriff's phone rang, and he glanced at the screen. "I have to take this," he said, turning away. He glanced over his shoulder. "I'll be right back. Don't do anything stupid while I'm gone."

Isaac snorted. "What do you expect me to do from inside here?" He gestured to the bars.

The sheriff's gaze moved to me. "I was talking to Jo." And then he speed walked toward the other end of the office as he answered the call.

I was proud that the sheriff was worried what I would do in his absence. It meant that I'd left an impression— that he recognized me as a go-getter. My attention returned to Isaac when he released a long sigh.

"What am I going to do, Jo? I've told the sheriff every- thing I can. And even though he can't prove I killed Bryce, he can't prove that I didn't kill him either."

"Innocent until proven guilty," I said. "Though Dottie tells me it tends to not be as cut and dried as all that. Human emotions and biases tend to muddy the waters."

Isaac perked up at that. "Dottie. She used to be a cop. Do you think she'd help me out?"

I hesitated, knowing that Dottie didn't like to get involved with investigations. Well, unless it was absolutely necessary. "You already have the sheriff working on your behalf," I said, my words slow. "He's good at what he does —looks at all the angles. You're in capable hands."

"But what if that's not enough?" Isaac asked. "He's under a lot of pressure, especially from the press. They're always hounding him, pressing him for new information. They run the same story over and over, with the addition of just one new fact or one new quote in each one. I've given him several names of people who I think could have done it, but he's skeptical. I suppose I would be too." Isaac's gaze moved to the window. It was on my side of the bars, so he likely didn't have a great view, but at least it was sunshine. "I'd give anything to put my feet in the ocean, if only for a few seconds."

I swore that man was part fish. Isaac didn't just like the ocean—he needed it. He needed that salty water, the breeze in his hair. Most young people his age had already left town in search of a brighter future for themselves, not wanting to be stuck running a tourist shop for the rest of their lives. But not Isaac. He was happy in his little bunga-low, lifeguarding by day and surfing by dawn and dusk.

And now he was trapped in this place.

"At least the press can't reach you in here, right?" I said.

Isaac nodded. "For now. They're getting more persistent by the hour. Especially this one reporter lady. She faked a sprained ankle right outside the building, and it almost worked. Deputy Randy was helping her inside when Sheriff Hart showed up and kicked her out." He paused. "Jo, would you please ask Dottie to visit me? I don't want her to investigate—I just need to ask her for advice."

I was still mad at Dottie, and the last thing I wanted to do right now was ask her for a favor. But looking at Isaac's sad face—how could I refuse?

"Of course. I'll have her here within the hour." I turned to leave, but then paused. "You mentioned that you gave the sheriff several names of potential suspects. Just out of curiosity, what names did you give him?"

Isaac slumped onto the bed. He looked exhausted, like he hadn't slept at all. "Told him to start with Michael Richards. He's another surfer, but knowing him, he's already skipped town. Bad sort of guy. Being a rebel is his brand, and he attracts a certain kind of fan. The ones that feel like they are on the outside looking in—never feeling like they've been part of the crowd. And the more Michael leans into that 'rebel without a cause' persona, the crazier his fans get. If he gave the word, I wouldn't put it past his fans to do the dirty work for him."

A crazy fan killing in the name of their idol. That was something we could work with.

8

I stood outside the bakery, staring at the back door to our apartment. It was hidden well enough that we didn't usually need to worry about unwanted visitors. But right now, it was me who felt like that unwanted visitor.

I was a burden to Dottie. Always had been. And even now, coming home, I was about to ask her to do something I knew would make her uncomfortable.

But it's not for you, I reminded myself. *It's for Isaac. He asked for Dottie.*

I opened the door and stepped into the long, dark hallway. If I continued forward, it would lead to the bakery. A staircase sat to my right, and it led to our upstairs apartment. I looked at it far longer than necessary, already exhausted and not looking forward to the climb. Staring at it wasn't going to get me upstairs, though, so I pushed through. It took a few minutes to get to the top, and I paused on the landing before letting myself through the second door. The one that mattered.

As soon as I entered the apartment, though, I knew something was wrong. It felt cold. Empty. Even before I searched the rooms, I knew I wouldn't find Dottie. She wasn't there.

All that climbing for nothing.

Maybe it was time that Dottie and I gave in and got cellphones. I could have called her directly from the sheriff's office and saved myself the trip.

I collapsed onto the living room couch, but even as my feet begged me to stay off them, I knew I couldn't. Dottie never went out on her own. Never went exploring. Like she'd said, her sole purpose was to protect me from myself. It always had been. When she'd become a cop, it was because she'd seen how I'd been treated when my kleptomania had gotten me into trouble. As young adults, when I'd told her I was moving away, she'd nearly followed me to New Mexico. We'd had a terrible fight when I'd told her that she was stifling me and the only reason I wanted to move away was because of her. She didn't follow me after that.

And now, here we were again.

Except this time, she had followed me. Or at least tried to. She'd likely left soon after I had but hadn't realized I'd taken the hidden path behind the shops.

Sisterly love was a strange thing.

I pushed myself up from the couch and lumbered

down the staircase once more, but this time exited through the front entrance, where I was more likely to find Dottie.

I was just rounding the corner to search the boardwalk when I saw Jessie. She and Patty, our local doctor, were having what looked like an animated conversation.

"Jo," Jessie exclaimed when she spotted me, abruptly cutting off her and Patty's conversation. "I am glad to see you."

I took in the two women. They both looked worried.

"What's wrong?" I asked. My mind jumped to all sorts of possibilities, the most prominent one being that the sheriff had found proof that Isaac really had killed Bryce. Or maybe I was the one being accused of murder—maybe they'd found poison in Autumn's bread pudding. I doubted that one was it—no one had that kind of bad luck, being accused of poisoning someone two murders in a row.

"It's Dottie," Jessie said.

My heart immediately constricted. "Where is she?"

"Resting in my clinic," Patty said. "She collapsed outside the scuba shop."

"What happened? It's not her heart, is it? Heart problems run in our family," I said, already turning and walking toward Patty's clinic.

"No, nothing as serious as that," Patty said. She and Jessie had no problem keeping up with me. "But I won't sugarcoat things, Jo. She's been pushing herself too hard, and if you ask me, so have you. I know you don't want to admit it, but you're getting older, and in my professional opinion, some changes need to be made."

No, I hadn't asked her. I didn't need her professional opinion to know that we were old. But we were doing fine, and our health was the best it had been in years.

My expression must have said so too, because Jessie rested her hand on my arm, and she gave me a kind smile. "She's not saying you need to stop going to parkour or going on your daily walks. And you certainly shouldn't close up the bakery. But you need to be aware of your limitations. Even I have had to make changes over the years."

Patty raised a finger. "Actually, I'm saying all of those things."

Jessie stopped walking and spun to face the doctor with a shocked expression. "You can't be serious. When Dottie first arrived, she had to use her cane one hundred percent of the time. Now she's only using it maybe seventy percent. With another year or two, we'll have her off it completely."

Patty chuckled, stopping next to Jessie. "Yes, and it sounds like you'll take personal offense if she isn't. But Dottie isn't a project to keep you busy. She's been doing too much. Running the bakery is a lot, but then you add in those blasted stairs they have to climb several times a day just to get to their apartment, not to mention the parkour and other activities—it's too much too quickly. They didn't get a chance to ease themselves into a more active lifestyle, and now it's taking a toll. Today, Dottie's heart was okay, but I can't make any guarantees for tomorrow."

I raised my hand, wondering if they remembered I was still there. "Can I have a say in this?"

They both looked at me, surprise etched in their faces. Yup, they'd forgotten me.

"Of course," Patty said.

"I agree about the horrendous stairs that lead up to our apartment," I said. "They're awful, and even though we have been getting fitter, just making it up to bed is a struggle. I don't see any solution to the problem, though, short of moving out of the bakery. And that's not something we can afford. Besides, we like living where we work. Makes us feel more comfortable that we're always there to keep an eye on things."

Patty raised a shoulder. "Well, you need to come up with something, because right now your sister is lying down in my office with a blood pressure cuff and an oxygen monitor."

And it had been all my fault she'd left the apartment, exhausted as she was.

Always the troublemaker.

THE MOMENT I walked into the examination room and saw Dottie lying on the bed, her eyes closed, I burst into tears, regret washing over me. "I'm sorry for the things I said. You were right, you're always taking care of me. I've been a burden since I was old enough to be one."

Dottie's eyes fluttered open, and it took a moment for them to focus on me. She gave me a weak smile. "You're not a burden—you're a gift. And you're my sister. I wouldn't have it any other way."

I approached her and took her hand. "You're not going to leave me?"

She released a quiet laugh. "Of course not. As much as your spontaneity gives me heart palpitations, I need you, and Autumn and the bakery, in my life. When we moved into the apartment together, you gave me so many things that I've been missing all these years." She paused. "I know I'm too rigid and you wish I'd loosen up a little bit. I'm trying, I really am."

If Dottie was saying she was trying to be more like me, that was a terrifying thought.

"Please, don't change," I said. "As unfair as it is to you, people like me need people like you to save us from ourselves. You're the yin to my yang, and I need that balance."

Dottie gave a single nod, no longer seeming burdened by the idea but refreshed by it. She shifted and used one arm to slowly push herself up until she was sitting. "I think I'm ready for my own bed now."

I thought back to Isaac—I'd promised I'd bring her to the sheriff's station, but that would be a terrible thing to do right now. Just as Dottie had looked after me all these years, I needed to do the same for her. I needed to protect her energy and her health, and forcing her into a murder investigation was not the way to do that.

I held out an arm, and Dottie grabbed hold, steadying herself. Once she looked like she wouldn't fall back over, I helped her take off the blood pressure cuff and the oxygen monitor.

"Do you want me to walk back to the bakery and get your car?" I asked.

She wrinkled her nose. "It's only a couple blocks away. I think I can manage that far with my cane. Seventy is the new sixty, you know."

I hadn't known, but this was promising. When we'd first moved here, Dottie had struggled to walk with her cane even on her good days, and she'd accepted it as fact that her body was falling apart. But this last year—she'd been fighting back. Unfortunately, her body had won this round, but I had no doubt that she'd win the match.

Patty bustled in just as I'd helped Dottie slip her shoes back on. Her concerned expression held a hint of panic. "What are you two doing? Dorothy, you need at least another good hour of rest and monitoring before you attempt to go anywhere."

Dottie gave the doctor a patient smile as I handed her her cane. "I appreciate you taking such good care of me, Patty. Thank you. But Jo will be with me, and our bakery is only a couple of streets away. I think my own bed is what I need right now."

Patty frowned. "Yes, but not those stairs. I mean, honestly, it's only going to get worse the older you get. They are brutal even for the young and healthy. I've heard Bree complaining about needing to climb up to their apartment above the scuba shop, and she's barely in her thirties. I can't imagine what it will be like when she and Caleb decide to have kids. Can you imagine doing those stairs pregnant?"

I couldn't, because I'd chosen to not have kids. There were times I wondered if I'd missed out on something—some grand life adventure I had been meant to have. But then I remembered all those times I'd interacted with the neighborhood youth, when a few minutes of fun was plenty and I was more than happy to send them home to their parents.

Of course, if I'd had kids of my own, they'd have been angels. Perfect in every way. And because they'd always be fictional, no one had the opportunity to prove otherwise.

"I can't imagine it," Dottie said. "And I will take your concerns to heart. Maybe Jo and I can look for a better living situation for ourselves."

Patty gave a hesitant nod, as if she hoped we really were considering it. "Well, if you feel well enough to walk, I can't keep you here. Just...be careful, okay? No parkour for a couple of weeks. Lots of rest, and make sure you're getting plenty of fluids."

Dottie waved a hand through the air. "Etcetera, etcetera. Yes, I'll do all the things."

"I'm serious," Patty said, following us out to the lobby. She looked at me. "Jo, I'm counting on you to make sure Dorothy is following doctor's orders and taking care of herself. No whisking her off on any adventures for a little while. I know how...spontaneous...you can be."

"I think the word you wanted to use was impulsive," I said with a smile. "And yes, I can certainly be that. But I'll walk Dottie home right now and tuck her into bed. Promise."

Patty looked like she wanted to believe me, but I could see that she had her doubts. "Dorothy, I want to see you back here in a week, just for a checkup."

Dottie looked like she was holding back an eye roll and merely said, "Yes, ma'am," as we exited the office.

"You go as slow as you need to," I told Dottie as we approached the sidewalk. "Patty makes a good point about those stairs, you know. One of these days they are going to kill us, and I really don't want that to be the way I go. Humiliating is what it would be."

Dottie chuckled. "I'm willing to examine what options we might have." She paused. "How is Isaac doing?"

Surprised by the question, I tripped on a crack in the sidewalk and nearly fell, and that wouldn't have been good for anyone. Patty would never let us leave her clinic again.

"Why do you ask?" I asked slowly.

"I saw you enter the sheriff's office," she said matter-of-factly. "The moment you left the apartment, I followed. Of course, you're quicker than I am, so I lost you for a while.

Didn't see you again until I saw you walking the boardwalk with Sheriff Hart. That was when my body failed me." She glanced down at her body, accusatory, like it had betrayed her. And then instead of turning right, which would be the quickest way home, she turned left.

"Where are you going?" I asked.

"The sheriff's station." Dottie paused to lean on her cane, taking in a couple of quick breaths. "It's just around the corner."

"Yes, but why? You should be resting. I promised Patty that I'd take you straight home."

Dottie chuckled. "Since when do you follow orders?" She straightened and began walking again. "You went to the sheriff's office, I'm assuming to check in on Isaac. You were also likely wanting to see if the sheriff had any new leads. If you want to get the answers you're looking for, you need to know the right questions to ask." She glanced at me. "Did you get the answers you were looking for?"

Sometimes I forgot how perceptive Dottie was. Her time on the police force had honed skills that I could never begin to imagine having.

I shook my head. "No. The sheriff took a call while I was there, but he left the room to talk. Isaac did say there was another surfer—a kind of renegade—that he could see being involved. I met that surfer briefly before the event, and he certainly has a fearless confidence about him. I don't think there's any evidence that ties him to the murder, though." I paused. "Why are you suddenly so interested in this investigation? You hate getting involved in these kinds of things. You say it's none of our business."

Dottie stopped again, taking a breathing break. "Because I can tell there's something you're keeping from me—something you want to say, but you are restraining yourself. You promised Patty that you'd take responsibility for me, and you're keeping that promise." Her gaze settled on me. "But if we can be a support to Isaac right now, we need to be. I've seen people locked up for months without receiving a single visitor. They didn't have any family—any friends. I know this isn't the same thing. Even though Isaac doesn't have any family here in town, he does have this entire crazy town making sure he's all right. Still, if I can be of any help to him—"

"He asked to see you," I blurted out. "Wants to ask your advice on the situation, I think."

"That's it? That's what you were keeping from me?" She released a relieved laugh. "I thought it was something far more serious than that. Of course I'd be happy to see him."

It could have been my imagination, but it seemed that Dottie's steps were a little lighter and a bit quicker. Not quick, by any means, but she took fewer breaks, anyway.

Ten minutes later, we were pushing our way through news crews that had appeared since I'd left. They'd positioned themselves around the sheriff's station, and they protested our pushing them aside. To my surprise, when they saw it was a couple of old women, their protests only got louder.

"Not a very nice group, is it?" I said to Dottie.

Regardless, we prevailed, and it didn't take long before we were standing inside the sheriff's station. Once the front doors closed behind us, however, we weren't met by the sheriff or Deputy Randy.

They were both far too preoccupied, their guns out and trained on a single man who had his hands up. On the man's right arm was a tattoo of a skeleton on a surfboard.

Michael Richards.

A gun sat on the ground midway between him and the sheriff.

And Isaac was nowhere to be seen.

9

D ottie grabbed my arm. "I think we should come back later," she whispered.

I fully agreed, and we retreated quickly as Sheriff Hart and Deputy Randy rushed toward the man.

"I didn't see Isaac," I said once we were outside, my breaths coming quick. Even though we were already out of harm's way, I still felt the need to keep my voice low. Dottie had warned me in the past about getting involved with investigations—she knew how messy they could get. And I pretended it was a game. *Let's see if we can get the murderer before the sheriff does. Let's see if we can find clues that he missed.*

And we had. We'd been instrumental in his past two murder investigations—mostly because we ourselves had had everything to gain and everything to lose.

That had been the problem, though. Because we'd

been successful, it had given me a confidence that wasn't good for me. And wasn't safe.

"Isaac looked like he was fine," Dottie said. "Scared, but okay. He was huddled in the far corner behind the bed."

That was a relief.

It was short-lived, however, because it didn't take more than a moment for microphones to be shoved in our faces and a barrage of questions to assault us.

"Don't say a thing," Dottie murmured, and she began whacking reporters who didn't get out of our way and allow us through.

A woman's voice rang out above them all. "You people are the ones who give reporters a bad name. Let them pass, for goodness' sake."

A woman in a business suit appeared in front of us and pushed aside the crowd, almost like she was our personal escort. I recognized her but was having trouble placing her. "Frank," she said, warning in her voice. "I swear if you don't lower that camera, I'm going to take it and add it to my collection."

The woman had beautiful dark hair and she patted it, as if to make sure it was still in place as we worked our way through the crowd.

Once we were through the thick of things, she stopped but gestured for us to continue walking. "If I were you, I wouldn't come back to the sheriff's station for a few days. Not with Michael Richards pulling a stunt like this. These people...they smell blood. They're no different than sharks, and they're circling."

Dottie snorted. "As if you aren't. Admit it, you helped us because you want to know what we saw in there."

The woman hesitated. "I would have helped regardless, but yes, I'm also interested in what you saw in there," she admitted. "All we know is that Michael Richards was waving a gun in the air as he sprinted down Main Street, and then he ran straight through the sheriff's doors. I can only imagine what was happening inside."

"Well, we're not going to tell you," Dottie said, then turned away. She motioned for me to follow.

I felt bad treating the woman this way after she'd just helped us, even if she was a reporter. I gave her a little wave as I followed Dottie. "Thank you for back there," I called to her. "We don't have the information you want, but we do make a lovely éclair. Come by Sandcastle Bakery, and we'll give you one. On the house, of course."

Dottie shot me an annoyed look, and I hurried after her. "You shouldn't have invited that vulture to our bakery. She was only being nice because she wanted something from us."

"Maybe, but every good action still deserves a reward, whatever her motives were."

Dottie was quiet for a moment. "Who do you think that Michael Richards fellow was?" she asked after sending a backward glance over her shoulder, likely making sure we weren't being followed. "A fan who blames Isaac for Bryce's death?"

I forgot that she hadn't met the rebel surfer.

"No. He's the renegade surfer I told you about—the one Isaac mentioned might be worth looking into. It looks like he was right."

Dottie looked more tired than ever as she struggled to keep up with my pace. "I hope the sheriff has more than that one jail cell, and preferably one that is separate from Isaac. For both of their sakes."

"It doesn't really make sense, though, does it?" I said. "Why would Michael show up at the sheriff's station with a gun if he was already getting away with murder? Everyone knew the sheriff had arrested Isaac for Bryce's death. Surely Michael wasn't after both Bryce and Isaac."

Dottie remained quiet, seeming lost in her own thoughts, and I shoved my hands into my pockets, still feeling a bit shaken. My right hand jammed into something.

It felt like a notebook.

I had a vague recollection of seeing the sheriff's note-book on the ground amid the chaos. I had scooped it up in the commotion. And stuck it in my pocket.

And then promptly forgotten I'd done it until now. That happened a lot. Forgetting. I'd tried so hard for so many years to overcome my kleptomania, and failed, that now when I did it, I often subconsciously blocked out the action. Until I rediscovered the object later. Sometimes I was able to stealthily return it. Other times, I would pretend I'd found it when I'd give it back.

And then there were the times when it had gotten me into serious trouble.

I was afraid that this would be one of those times.

"Uh...Dottie?" I said, fingering the pages but not daring to pull the notebook out. My steps slowed until I stopped.

She tossed me a curious glance. "What is it?"

"We need to go back to the sheriff's station." My entire body tightened as I waited for her response. I knew she wouldn't reprimand me for taking something—she knew it wasn't my fault—but there was always that flicker of disappointment. She tried to hide it—didn't want me to feel bad. But it was always there.

It made me wonder why Dottie had agreed to open the bakery with me, knowing what she'd have to put herself through. She had been right when she'd said that some things never change. It was our teenage years all over again.

But rather than disappointed, Dottie looked quizzical. "Did you think of something the sheriff ought to know about?"

I hesitated, then shook my head.

"You took something." It was a statement this time, not a question.

I gave a little nod.

Still no disappointment.

"What did you take?" she asked.

"The sheriff's notebook that he always keeps in his pocket. It must have fallen out during the exchange with Michael Richards. He'll know it's missing—he takes it everywhere. If I return it quickly enough, maybe he won't notice."

Dottie tilted her head to the side. "Interesting." She held out a hand. "May I have a look?"

My straight-as-they-come sister wanted to look at the sheriff's investigation notes? When I didn't move right away, she waved her hand impatiently. "Quickly, please. That is, if you want to return the sheriff's notebook before he traces it back to you."

That got me moving.

I pulled it out and placed it into her hand with one swift motion.

Dottie glanced at the page it had been open to, then flipped back a couple of pages. Her nose scrunched and then it relaxed, and she murmured, "Yes, that makes sense." She glanced at me. "I always wondered what the sheriff's process was. Everyone is different, of course— their own unique style of thinking about things and organizing their thoughts. When I was on the force, I rarely wrote more than a single word, and yet it would mean the same thing as a full page. Only I'd be able to decipher it, so I was never worried about others reading it."

She handed me back the notebook. "He is very organized and thorough. It's almost like reading a novel—a fictionalized version of what could have happened."

"And what could have happened?" I asked, not waiting for her answer as I skimmed over the pages.

"I'm not the fastest reader in the world, so I didn't get through it all," she said. "But from what I did read, the sheriff doesn't think Isaac did it, which is a relief. What confuses me is why Sheriff Hart has his sights set on the girlfriend. He says he's close to finding the proof he needs and he doesn't want to scare her off. But I don't know that I'm convinced Felicity did it. She was sitting with us right up until Bryce competed."

I flipped back another few pages and speed read. Growing up, I had been able to read an entire novel in less than an hour. My mom had thought I was doing myself a disservice back then, but it sure was coming in handy now.

"It's because of the belladonna berries."

"The what?" Dottie asked

"Belladonna berries. It's a very poisonous plant—"

Dottie held up a hand, stopping me. "Yes, I know what it is. But are you saying that that is what killed Bryce Carlton?"

"Yes. They found remnants of the berries in his stomach, and they'd only recently been eaten. Do you remember Felicity telling Bryce that he needed to eat the oatmeal she'd set out for him?"

Dottie's lips parted in surprise. "And that there were extra berries, because he needed the energy for his big day." She gave a sad shake of her head. "I really liked her."

I slipped the notebook back into my pocket. "The

sheriff didn't mention any other suspects, but even with the berries, I don't think it was Felicity."

Dottie and I turned back to the sheriff's office, and we walked in silence until we reached the group of reporters —they were all still there.

"How are we going to make it back inside?" I whispered. "We barely made it through the cameras last time."

Before Dottie could answer, the front door to the station flew open. "Isaac," I yelped in surprise. He stood before us, looking tired but unscathed. The cameras swooped in, and before I could think better of it, I elbowed my way to him.

"Give the man some space," I shouted.

Dottie followed and positioned herself on the other side of him as we escorted him through the crowd. Once we had some breathing room, I wrapped my arms around him, giving the biggest hug I could manage. He laughed as I stepped back and then whacked him on the arm.

"You scared us, you know, getting yourself arrested like that."

Isaac gave me his signature lopsided grin—I hadn't realized how much I'd missed it until this moment, and my eyes welled up with moisture.

"Oh, no need to cry for me, Jo," he said, pulling me in for a side hug. "I'm all right. You remember that surfer I told you about, Michael Richards? He burst into the sheriff's station wanting to enact vengeance for Bryce's death. Had a gun and everything. If you ask me, it was a publicity stunt, but the sheriff has only one cell, so he arrested Michael and then let me go on the condition that I don't leave town."

Dottie and I blinked.

"I'm sorry, say that again?" Dottie said. "You think that Michael stormed into the sheriff's station, with a gun, as a publicity stunt?"

The way Dottie had described Isaac huddling in his cell when we'd escaped the scene—in that moment, he'd thought it all had been very real.

"Well, sure," he said. "The cameras are already here, everywhere we go. From the way the sheriff was complaining, the number of news crews has doubled since Bryce's death, and Michael loves an audience. It helps his image of the rebel surfer and only gets him more fans, especially if he's certain the sheriff can't pin Bryce's death on him." He shook his head, though, as if there was no way that was an actual possibility.

"It could have been for publicity," I said slowly, "but no reporters were allowed inside the station."

Isaac's lips twitched up, like he was fighting a smile. "Yes, but from what I heard, he ran down Main Street waving that gun, right? He was the reason all of the reporters were gathered on the sheriff's steps—they'd followed him. And now he's counting on me telling everyone what happened inside the sheriff's station; it's no good if he tells people himself. He figures I'll tell the story of how he burst into the station, gun waving, demanding justice for Bryce Carlton. It doesn't matter how I try to spin it—even if I told people that Michael has lost his mind and that he tried to kill me, he comes off as the hero. The vigilante. And then the news crews will beg to interview Michael to get his side of the story and find out what really happened. When the sheriff says he's unavailable for an interview, the news stations will weasel the story from Deputy Randy, and that will only further solidify Michael's place with his crazy fans. I swear, they think of him as untouchable—they think of him like a god."

I didn't know if all surfers were like this, but the number of rivalries Isaac had—and the person they had turned him into—I didn't like it. I preferred our Isaac when it had been just him and his love of water.

"If you already know what's going to happen, why do you look so happy about it?" Dottie asked.

Isaac grinned. "Because I'm not going to tell a single soul about what went on in there. Michael is going to wait and wait, expecting his adoring fans to storm the castle at any moment, but there will be nothing but crickets. It will have all been for nothing."

The way Isaac looked so giddy in that moment—I definitely didn't like this version of our local surfer.

"Well I, for one, am glad to know that we missed the excitement," Dottie said, acting like we hadn't walked right into the middle of the standoff. She threw a quick glance at the sheriff's station. "Jo mentioned to me that you were hoping to ask my advice on your situation. Are you still wanting to talk?" Her gaze returned to Isaac. "I'm happy to help any way I can."

Isaac seemed surprised that we weren't nearly as enthralled with Michael's imminent fall from grace as he was, and then that surprise morphed into embarrassment. "I think I'm okay for now, but thank you for coming all the way down here. I hope it wasn't too much of an inconvenience."

Dottie smiled. "Of course not. I'm just thrilled you're no longer cooped up in that jail cell." Her eyes flickered toward the sheriff's station once more, and she was no doubt thinking about the time restraint we had in returning that notebook. "I'm sorry to run off, Isaac, but we need to have a quick word with the sheriff. Please let me know if you need anything, though. Anything at all."

He stepped aside and held out an arm, gesturing for us to continue. "Of course. And thank you."

I took his hand and patted it as we passed him. "It's very nice to see you out and about. Let's do our best to keep it that way."

"I'll do my best," Isaac said, then, with a final wave, he hurried away before any reporters could block his exit.

Dottie and I were getting used to the press by now and had figured out a strategy to get through the crowd without too much trouble. First step was to ignore their questions, and the second step included sharp elbows, which both Dottie and I had been blessed with.

When the sheriff's door shut behind us, I immediately

scanned the room, looking for the best place to deposit the notebook. Sheriff Hart and Randy were in a far corner, talking in whispers. Michael Richards was prancing around in his cell, singing "Yellow Submarine" by the Beatles at the top of his lungs. He seemed drunk, which wouldn't have surprised me at all. I had a feeling his tune was going to change once he'd slept that off.

Now was the perfect time to return the notebook without the sheriff noticing. I approached his desk, but just as I slipped the notebook from my pocket, Sheriff Hart said:

"Jo and Dorothy. I didn't hear you come in." He paused and glanced toward Michael. "For obvious reasons."

I froze and looked up. The sheriff was all smiles as he and Randy approached us. I now had a dilemma. Drop the notebook so he'd find it later on the floor, or toss it quickly onto a stack of papers on the desk.

With all the racket from Michael Richards, my mind wasn't able to process quickly enough, and the sheriff saw the notebook before I could implement either plan.

His smile disappeared.

10

Sheriff Hart's lips pulled into a frown. "Jo, what are you doing with my notebook?"

I threw a panicked glance at Dottie, but she looked completely nonplussed. "You dropped it. We found it on the floor when we walked in." My sister then sent me a look that said, *You're fine. Play along and just give him back the notebook.*

At least, that was what I thought her look meant. I was very good at reading her mood but not so great at reading her thoughts.

I held out the notebook to the sheriff. "You really should be more careful with it. Any old person could have picked it up—you're just lucky it was us."

Sheriff Hart studied me. "Yes, Lucky." He took the notebook. "So, tell me, Dorothy," he said while fingering the pages. His gaze jumped to my sister. "What did you make of my deductions? Would you have drawn the same conclusions when you were on the force?"

The sheriff hadn't been fooled in the slightest by our attempt to return the notebook. It probably didn't help that he knew about my kleptomania from a previous investigation.

Dottie opened her mouth to speak but then closed it again. I thought this must have been the only time I'd seen her truly speechless. Dottie raised a shoulder, evidently giving up the ruse.

"Back then, yes, I would have."

Sheriff Hart nodded slowly. "But now?"

Dottie hesitated. "The evidence of the poisonous berries in conjunction with the oatmeal makes Felicity your most viable suspect."

Michael Richards overheard the conversation and shouted from the cell, "What about me? I'd make a pretty good suspect. Brought a gun and everything."

"I thought you were avenging Bryce's death, but now you're saying that you killed him?" I called back.

Deputy Randy winced. "Don't encourage him. We figure if he doesn't have an audience, then he'll settle down. At least that's what we're hoping. I can't listen to 'Yellow Submarine' for the next seven hours."

"That's what I wanted you to think," Michael yelled, though we would have been able to hear him just fine if he'd talked normally. "Bryce wasn't cheating, by the way. But no one will believe me. I can't say the same thing about

Judge Pence. A disgrace to the surfing community. He's going to be next, you know." Michael started twirling in circles and singing, "Victor Pence, dead as a fence." On repeat.

"At least it's not 'Yellow Submarine,'" Dottie said dryly.

Randy closed his eyes and massaged his temples. "Now that he's threatened someone else, he really isn't going anywhere for a while. I almost wish Felicity did do it, just so we can let this guy go. She seems like she'd be the quiet type."

Dottie frowned. "You want Felicity to be guilty of murder just so you don't have to listen to a drunk surfer?"

"When you put it that way, you make it sound like I'm a terrible person," Randy said. "But if I snap before we're done with this guy and do something I'll later regret, you'll remember this moment."

"Save yourself the trouble and buy some earplugs." Dottie gave an annoyed harrumph. "Felicity as a suspect makes sense, and you certainly need to question her, but have you looked into this judge, Victor Pence?"

Randy glanced at the sheriff, letting him take this one. Apparently, this had been something they'd discussed, but they didn't necessarily want us privy to how that conversation had gone.

"We are considering all angles," the sheriff finally said. "Now, if you'll excuse us, we have some work to do."

That was our cue to leave, and our mission of returning the stolen notebook had been accomplished, so

I gave the sheriff a small salute and turned toward the door.

"Oh, and Jo?" the sheriff said.

I paused.

"You don't have anything else of mine in those pockets of yours, do you?"

I didn't think I'd stolen anything this time, as my sole focus had been on returning the last thing I'd stolen. But just in case, and to put the sheriff's mind at ease, I patted my pockets and turned them inside out. "Empty," I said, and then left the office before he could arrest me for theft.

"WHAT DO YOU THINK?" I asked Dottie the moment we'd walked around the corner where the reporters could no longer see us.

She closed her eyes and tilted her head up to the sun, relishing the warmth. She did that a lot, and it always brought a smile to her face. "That I'm very glad Isaac is free. We can trust the sheriff to do his due diligence moving forward."

Meaning now that Isaac was no longer locked up, she didn't feel the need to be involved. She didn't care which one of the others had done it, and she didn't feel like I should care either.

"I suppose you're right," I said. "That Michael guy is off his rocker. I wouldn't be surprised if he was telling the truth and he really did kill Bryce."

We turned another corner to head back to the bakery and nearly collided with a man holding a camera. A woman in a business suit stood next to him. It was the reporter who had helped us escape the sheriff's office earlier.

Her expression brightened when she saw us. "I saw your bakery was closed and hoped I'd run into you."

"We don't have anything to say to you," Dottie said, her words crisp and to the point.

"Of course not," the reporter said, following us as we continued walking toward the bakery. "You did offer me éclairs, though, and I thought I'd stop by in between news updates and take you up on your kind offer."

Dottie didn't bother slowing down. "We sold out and won't open until tomorrow. You can try again then."

I rested a hand on Dottie's shoulder, slowing her down. "The woman has been nothing but nice to us," I said, my voice low. "The least you could do is be nice back."

"I don't blame you for not trusting my motives," the reporter said from behind us. "I'm not going to pressure you to talk about what happened at the sheriff's station, if that's what you're worried about."

Dottie turned to face her, and I followed suit. "Then what is it that you are going to pressure us to talk about?"

The reporter hesitated, likely knowing this was her one and only chance at getting into Dottie's good graces. "The thing is, the other day I saw your sister talking with Bryce Carlton," she said, her words slow. "Right before the competition when she walked off with his girlfriend, Felicity Andrews." She turned to me. "You two seemed awfully friendly, especially considering you're a local. Are you a fan of Bryce Carlton?"

That was where I'd seen her before. She had been watching Felicity and me on the beach. I immediately put my guard up. The reporter was still all smiles—but I realized, though I couldn't put my finger on what it was exactly, there was something off-putting that Dottie must have sensed from the very beginning. I needed to trust my sister's instincts more often.

I smiled. "No. We're team Isaac all the way." I paused. "What did you say your name was?"

The reporter's smile widened, and she stuck out a hand. "Juliette Bigsby." She glanced at her phone. "I'm sorry to have to cut the conversation short, but we're about to go live with some updates on the murder investigation." She paused, her gaze scrutinizing as it returned to us. "You know, we haven't had the chance to chat with any locals. I'd love to interview you as part of the segment, if you're up for it. You know, get a different perspective. Someone from team Isaac." She said it as if she'd just realized this, but her acting needed some work.

We didn't answer quickly enough, and Juliette took that to mean we would love to be on whatever national news channel she was from.

Juliette turned to the camera and flashed a bright

smile. Her cameraman held up three fingers, lowered each as he counted down, then pointed at her.

"Thanks, John," Juliette said. "You'd think that things would be settling down here in the quiet town of Starlight Ridge since the murder of surfing legend Bryce Carlton, but it's been quite the opposite. I'm here with two local women who have some strong opinions on what has been going on."

"I wouldn't say that strong is the correct—" Dottie started, but Juliette cut her off.

"Your local sheriff has been keeping all visitors at arm's length," Juliette said. "He has, however, released local hero Isaac Larson and instead arrested Michael Richards for the murder of Bryce Carlton. Do you have any theories on why he released Isaac and arrested an out-of-towner instead? Seems we may need to bring in someone more objective to take over this murder investigation. I mean, it was Isaac who purposely knocked Bryce off his surfboard. We all saw it. And yet, every local person we've talked to in this town defends Isaac, regardless of the evidence."

I knew this tactic. Juliette, as nice as she'd seemed outside the sheriff's office, was leading us into a trap. She was trying to get us to defend the sheriff, expecting that we'd somehow bumble into admitting that our sheriff wasn't as objective as he should be. I glanced at the camera, the little red light on, as the entire country awaited our answer.

Dottie placed a hand on my shoulder—a warning not to say anything.

She then straightened, faced Juliette, and smiled. "I am Dorothy Darby, and this is my sister, Jo. We don't know anything about murder, but we do know a thing or two about desserts that are so delicious, they're to die for. Jo and I own Sandcastle Bakery, where you can find all your favorite French pastries. We have everything from dacquoise and bread pudding to éclairs and macarons. Just follow the boardwalk, turn left, and we're three shops up. Once again, that's Sandcastle Bakery. We open tomorrow morning at ten. Mention that you heard about us here, and you'll receive a ten percent discount."

And then she just stood there, smiling like a fool, waiting for the news crew to cut away. So I followed suit and grinned at the camera.

Juliette and her cameraman didn't seem to know how to gracefully recover from that, so she quickly ended the segment by saying their audience could get all the latest updates on whichever channel it was that they were representing.

As soon as the light on the camera blinked off, Juliette rounded on us. "What was that?" she said angrily. "You made me look like an idiot on national television."

"Oh no, you did that yourself, dear," Dottie said, turning up the innocent old woman routine we'd perfected. It was necessary the moment a person hit sixty years old—

we all had to learn it. "You tried to 'lead the witness,' so to speak. There were a number of ways you could have recovered from our little advertisement. For instance, you could have asked if Bryce Carlton or Michael Richards, or any of the other surfers, had had a chance to try our pastries."

"That's just more advertising for your bakery," the reporter spat out.

"True," Dottie said. "But then you would be leading the conversation back to the surfers. And in doing so, you would have discovered that Jo had offered Bryce some bread pudding to wish him luck just before the competition, but he wouldn't even speak to her, let alone eat our bread pudding. His girlfriend, Felicity, ate it instead. We were with her when the accident occurred."

Juliette stared. "That would have made a great segment, and you held out on me. On purpose."

"No, we wanted you to do your job," Dottie said. "It's not our fault you let a couple of elderly women throw you off your game." And then Dottie linked her arm through mine and led me away. "Come along, Jo. We have a bakery to run."

When we were sure to be out of earshot, I said, "You never would have told her all of those things on live television, no matter the questions she asked."

Dottie grinned. "No, I wouldn't have. But it will drive that woman bonkers thinking that she just missed out on a golden opportunity."

I glanced at my sister. "That's not like you—messing with her like that. It's mean."

"To you, the kindest person on the planet, it probably seems like it is," Dottie said. "But I've dealt with my share of reporters over the years, and they're vultures, all of them. They look for a dying animal, then all of them circle. And to that reporter, we were the fresh carcass. We were her next meal. She was only nice to us outside the sheriff's station because she wanted information from us. If anything, I taught her a valuable lesson that I hope she'll take with her when she leaves Starlight Ridge."

"And what lesson is that?" I asked, stopping in front of the bakery.

"Never underestimate anyone, no matter their age." She paused and glanced at me. "We embarrassed her, and she knows where we work, which means she'll be paying us a visit, and this time it won't be on live television. Women like her always need to have the last word— always need the upper hand. Once she does, we'll really be able to get to the meat of things."

I raised an eyebrow. "You want her to visit us. But why? You said you were finished with this investigation, now that Isaac has been released."

Dottie unlocked the front door. "Because that woman is dangerous. If she starts getting it into people's heads that our sheriff is protecting his own, they might bring in outside law enforcement—people who only look at the surface and jump to the easiest conclusions. That wouldn't be good for Isaac or any of us. If she meets us here at the bakery, we can have a nice, informal conversation over pastry and clear the air."

"There will always be more reporters," I said, following her inside.

Dottie locked the front door behind us. "True. But this is the only one I'm worried about. On the inside of her wrist, she has a tattoo of a manatee."

"I didn't notice it," I said. "Let me guess, it looks eerily similar to the one on Bryce's surfboard.

Dottie nodded. "Exactly like the one on his surfboard."

11

I had complete faith in my older sister—I always had. But I had to admit that I wondered if Dottie had misread the situation. Free advertising for the bakery was one thing, but expecting that reporter to return after what Dottie had done—I had my doubts.

"You need to warn me the next time you pull a stunt like that," Autumn said the next morning, bringing out another tray of dacquoise as I flipped the OPEN sign. "When I saw you two on the news yesterday, I nearly had a heart attack, knowing what it would mean for me. You two said I could have yesterday off to relax."

"That was my fault," Dottie said. She sat on a stool behind the display counter as she petted Skittles. "That reporter means to cause trouble, and we need to stop her before she has the chance."

Autumn was right to be nervous about what that ad

would do for our bakery. Almost everyone who purchased pastries over the next few hours mentioned the ad on TV, wanting the ten percent discount. It had been a brilliant move on Dottie's part. It wasn't so great for Autumn, and we quickly ran out of pastries. It was impossible for her to bake as fast as we were selling them. I didn't mind. The earlier we sold out, the earlier we could close up and I could go to bed.

Except, Juliette Bigsby didn't show up like Dottie had thought she would.

All afternoon my gaze kept jumping to the window. I expected her to be there, watching—waiting for the perfect opportunity to confront us.

"She's not going to come," I told Dottie as I flipped the CLOSED sign. "She likely wants nothing to do with us."

"Tomorrow," Dottie said, confident as she counted the money in the till and placed the cash in a large envelope. We'd put it in the safe for the evening and take it to the bank in the morning.

I sat down across from her at the counter. "I'm sure plenty of people have manatee tattoos. She might not be connected to Bryce at all. Just annoyed that we wasted her time."

But then a knock on the front door startled us, and I turned.

I should have known that Dottie would be right about the reporter. My sister had amazing instincts that had served her well on the police force, and those instincts hadn't diminished with age.

"I'm sorry for doubting you," I said, pushing myself up from the stool. "What are you going to do if her camera guy is with her?"

"He won't be," Dottie said, placing the money in the safe that was hidden behind the counter. At first glance, it looked like it was part of a cabinet, blending seamlessly with the surrounding wood. Another byproduct of Dottie's days on the force—always being prepared.

I unlocked the front door and scanned the road in front of the bakery. It was deserted. The reporter was indeed alone.

Once again, Dottie had been right.

"We're closed," I said, not opening the door more than a couple of inches and pretending to misunderstand Juliette's intentions for visiting the bakery. "I'm sorry you keep missing out on those éclairs I promised you, but we'll open again at ten o'clock tomorrow morning."

"I'm not here for pastries," the reporter said. "I think we got off on the wrong foot, and I'm here to apologize."

Well, that was unexpected.

"Wonderful," I said. "Go ahead, then."

Juliette hesitated. "Mind if I come in and do it in there?"

I glanced back at Dottie, as if we hadn't already planned on Juliette joining us. I turned back. "All right. But make it quick. We have an early bedtime." I ushered her in, then locked the door behind her.

Juliette's previously perfect locks of brown hair were now disheveled, her beautiful pantsuit exchanged for jeans and a fitted T-shirt.

"I'd like to start over," she said, then she stuck out a hand. "Hi, I'm Juliette Bigsby. It's a pleasure to make your acquaintance."

Before I could introduce myself, Dottie intervened. "Is that your real name?" She leaned on the counter, her gaze intense.

Juliette hesitated. "No," she finally admitted. "When I was starting out, the stations who interviewed me didn't like the idea of introducing a Margaret Hayes. As soon as I changed my name to Juliette, the offers started rolling in." She looked a bit sad at the thought, but then perked right back up, as she'd been trained to do. "Only my family calls me Margaret now."

"Would you mind if we did?" I asked kindly. It had to be so difficult to have to change your entire identity just to be taken seriously. She might have been the best reporter in the entire country, but no one would have ever known based on the one thing that Margaret hadn't had any control over—her name.

Her expression grew serious. "I'd prefer if you didn't. I'm Juliette. Even to my friends." Her eyes softened. "And I do hope that we can be friends."

I didn't know if this was an act or not—given the

nature of her job, it very well could be. But we could act too, and we needed to know what information Juliette had. If it was harmless stuff that couldn't hurt Isaac or the town, great. She could go on her way, and we could breathe easy.

If not...

"Juliette," I said with a smile. "We've sold out of most everything, but I might be able to find a stray macaron in the back. Would you like one?"

Dottie held up a finger as she eyed the reporter. "Just a moment, Jo. She still hasn't apologized."

Looked like we were back to the good cop, bad cop routine. It had worked well for us in the past, so I supposed there was no harm in continuing with the status quo.

"That's right," I said, turning back to Juliette. "You go ahead and apologize, then I'll get the pastries and we can celebrate our new friendship."

She looked taken aback, being put on the spot like that, but then she nodded and pulled in a long breath. "Yesterday, I wanted you to admit that not only are you two biased, but your entire town is. That you'll do anything to protect your own. That wasn't fair of me, and I'm sorry."

I smiled and clapped my hands together. "What a lovely apology. That works for me. I'll get the—"

"Jo, relax for a minute, will you?" Dottie interrupted, sounding exasperated.

My smile dipped. "I'm sorry, Dottie. It's just that she gave a very nice apology, and I could use a macaron myself."

Dottie's facade slipped for a brief moment, a smile breaking through, but it disappeared just as fast. "I understand, but she's only sorry because we turned her news segment into an advertisement for the bakery. She's like all the rest of the reporters crawling around this town, looking for any scraps of new information they can find. She doesn't care about us—she cares about her own self-preservation."

Dottie turned her attention to Juliette. "I appreciate you taking the time to come here and apologize, but I think you need to leave now. Like Jo said, it's nearing our bedtime."

Juliette pulled out her phone and glanced at the screen. "But it's only four-thirty."

Oh, right. We had closed early.

Dottie didn't let that affect her in the slightest. Instead, she raised an eyebrow. "Yes, and?"

Juliette opened her mouth as if to say something, but then closed it.

"Was there something else, or shall I unlock the door for you?" I asked with a chipper smile. As if I wasn't thinking about the macarons I so desperately wanted to bring out and share, if for no other reason than to satisfy my own craving.

A beat of silence, and then Juliette's pleasant demeanor dropped and her eyes narrowed. "Bryce Carlton didn't deserve the ending he got, and Isaac is responsible. I asked for this assignment, even though it was a fluff piece. I had to see Bryce in person. He's masterful at everything he does." She caught herself using the present tense and corrected herself. "When he was out on those waves, he was like an artist, making them his own. I know about the rumors that he cheated, but it isn't true. I've researched it from every angle and talked to everyone that has anything to do with these competitions. It was impossible."

"Impossible to buy off a judge?" I asked. "Everyone has their price."

Juliette was already shaking her head. "But there are checks and balances to ensure that can't happen. The final score is the average of several judges' scores. You're saying he bought off all of them, and not one of them gained a conscience?"

That did seem unlikely.

"What about the head judge?" Dottie asked. "Couldn't he have swayed it slightly in Bryce's direction?"

Juliette released a cannon-like laugh. "Victor Pence? No, he didn't get where he did by accepting bribes. He's as straight as they come, and as knowledgeable as they come too. He surfed competitively when he was younger, but after he was injured, he decided not to return to the sport. Not a day after he retired, he was being recruited as a judge." She paused. "What I'm trying to say is, Bryce was a good guy. He didn't deserve the ending he got. I mean, poisoned by berries? If Bryce was going to leave the Earth early—and he always said he meant to—it was going to be doing the thing he loved most in the world. The ocean was the only thing that was strong enough to take him—or so I had thought."

Juliette's voice hitched on the last part, and her eyes welled up.

She seemed genuine. So much so that tears sprang to my own eyes.

Here was a man that so many had thought was invincible.

And yet, he had been killed so easily.

"You seem to know a lot about Bryce," I said. "What do you know of his upbringing? I'm assuming he grew up on the coast, surfing since he was a toddler."

What I really wanted to know was if he had a history with people here at the competition that we didn't know about.

"He lived on the west coast, but he didn't grow up surfing like you'd expect," Juliette said. "Bryce didn't learn until he was seventeen years old."

She paused and acted like she was waiting for a reaction.

"Wow, good for him," I finally said.

Juliette released a sigh and shook her head, like I didn't understand what she was trying to convey. "That is incredibly late for a competitive surfer. It means that every other surfer out there had at least a decade of experience more than Bryce had. Next week would have been his twenty-fifth birthday. To go from zero to best in the world in less than seven years is amazing. He was a natural. So of course the other surfers hated him. They were jealous. For the same reason that we all loved him."

"We?" Dottie asked, pushing away from the counter.

Juliette blinked, her eyes widening, like she'd said something she shouldn't have, and she shifted nervously. "You know, I've kept you too long," she said, backing toward the door. "I appreciate you letting me apologize, though. I really do feel bad about earlier."

I didn't move to unlock the door, because I knew exactly what Dottie had realized.

"You're not just a reporter who loves surfing," I said. "You have a tattoo that matches Bryce's surfboard, and you referred to yourself as part of a collective."

Dottie nodded. "You were in his fan club."

Juliette hesitated but ultimately relented. "Not that I could ever admit it—it wouldn't help my career, as you can imagine. And we're not a fan club. That implies we're starstruck teenagers with a celebrity crush. We're supporters. We interact on forums and the like, even made Bryce cards wishing him good luck." She puffed out her chest. "I was able to hand-deliver them the night before the competition. Best moment of my life was when I was able to walk up to him, look him in the eyes, and tell him that we were all rooting for him."

I smiled. "What a special moment. Did he love the cards as much as you hoped he would?"

Juliette returned my smile. "He loved them more. I even got a selfie with him—it was incredible." She pulled out her phone once more, glancing at the screen. "I've kept you too long." She looked at me. "I know you love Isaac, but Bryce deserves justice, no matter where it lands. You can't protect your own just because it feels good." And then she nodded to the front door. "Mind letting me out?"

"Of course." I took a moment to fumble with the keys. "I have one last question," I said, approaching the door. I let the keys slip from my fingers, and they landed on the tile floor with a loud clatter. Skittles immediately jumped from the counter, eyeing the keys as her new plaything. "What do you know about Bryce's coach?"

I bent over to pick up the keys, but not before seeing the anger that flitted across Juliette's face. By the time I had straightened, her smile was back.

"Lindi Fierce. Lovely woman, from what I can tell. Always had Bryce's best interests in mind," Juliette said. "Of course, I've heard it both ways."

"Both ways?" Dottie asked as I unlocked the door. I tried taking my time, but I didn't think that Juliette would believe that it took more than a couple of minutes to do it. Skittles had made her way over to me and was looking up expectantly, hoping I'd drop the keys again.

Juliette's smile never faltered as she said, "Yes. I've never seen it myself, of course, but from the way I hear it, she can have quite the temper. But like I said, she always did what was best for Bryce. He was the world champion, after all. Can't complain about that."

Juliette said it as she reached forward and turned the

key the rest of the way for me. "This is a tricky door, isn't it." And then she left before I could say more.

"Interesting woman," Dottie said, leaning on the counter, looking thoughtful.

I locked the door again. "Yes. A reporter who is obsessed with Bryce Carlton. That doesn't bode well for our sheriff, does it? I know you don't want to admit it, Dottie, but I think he may need our help."

12

I barely slept that night, my mind rehashing the encounter with Juliette over and over again. Rather than attempt to fight the impossible situation, I got up early, intent on visiting Sheriff Hart before we needed to open the bakery at ten o'clock.

Convincing Dottie to come with me would be an entirely different matter.

"You okay?" Dottie asked, rubbing her bloodshot eyes as she stumbled from her room. "I heard you tossing and turning all night."

"I heard you as well," I said. "You got up to use the bathroom four times—twice as much as your usual two." I reached into a box that I had set on the table and pulled out a leash. "That's why I'm getting Skittles ready for her morning walk. We could use the fresh air to wake us up before starting our busy day, and I thought breakfast at the diner might be nice."

Dottie cocked her head to the side, as if wondering if she was truly awake. "We've never taken Skittles on a walk. I didn't even know we had a leash."

"I bought it a few months ago, but tourist season was much busier than I had expected, and it's been sitting in my closet ever since."

"Absolutely not," Dottie said. "Skittles will never stand for it."

"You don't know that." I untangled the leash, realizing there was a harness that needed to clip around the cat's midsection. Dottie might be right about this being a bad idea—there was no way Skittles was going to sit still and let us put this thing on her. More likely than not, I would need first aid by the time I was finished.

That wasn't going to stop me from trying, though—especially because Dottie was so convinced that I couldn't do it.

I glanced around the kitchen. "Where is that cat, anyway?"

"Sleeping still," Dottie said. "I don't think she liked being woken as many times as she was last night."

Perfect. A sleeping cat was a tame cat. Usually.

"Don't you dare wake her up," Dottie warned. "That's my bedroom, and you're not allowed in."

And all of a sudden I was thirteen again, being banned from my sister's room. Dottie's warnings had never been enough to keep me out then—it was funny that she thought it was enough now.

After making certain I had the harness ready, I crept into Dottie's room, her protests now whispers as she followed me.

"You have no right," she whispered angrily.

I ignored her.

There Skittles was, lounging in the middle of Dottie's bed. As soon as I sat on the edge, her eyes opened. They were sleepy eyes, though, and I lifted her, moving the harness into place as I did so. What I hadn't counted on was her stretching, then clinging to the comforter.

"Let go, sweet Skittles," I said, clipping the harness into place. I reached over and picked her up, but the more I pulled, the more her claws seemed to grip the blanket. I sucked in a quick breath when I heard a tear.

"That's it, you owe me a new comforter," Dottie said, taking Skittles from my arms. "I hope your attempt at proving me wrong was worth it."

"It was," I said calmly, then picked up the end of the leash. "Now, if you'll excuse me, I have a cat to feed, then we are going on our walk."

Dottie's eyes held fire, but then they softened. "All right. This I have to see." She set Skittles down, and the cat immediately rushed forward toward the kitchen. Thankfully, I'd had enough time to plant my feet and grab the leash's loop with both hands. The cat bounced back with a yelp, and she glared at me.

"She doesn't like it," Dottie said, wearing a smug smile. She took the leash from me. "Now, if you don't mind..."

She bent down to remove the harness, but I snatched the leash out of her hands and gave a soft pull, and Skittles complied, walking just out of Dottie's reach.

"She has to get used to it."

After that, Skittles gave me no more trouble, following me to the kitchen where she had her breakfast, and then down the stairs like the good cat she was.

"Now she can get all that fresh air and sunshine, but with us in control," I said, moving toward the back door. "We don't want her wandering around with all these tourists and reporters parading about."

Even Dottie couldn't argue with that logic. And so, like Skittles, my sister followed me outside. Exactly how I'd intended.

Of course, if Dottie had known I wasn't merely out for a walk to get some breakfast, she would have locked the doors and swallowed the key, and none of us would have had our morning walk.

As it was, though, once we were outside, Dottie's steps quickened, and she breathed in a lungful of the salty air that we were blessed with each and every day. She smiled as Skittles ran ahead—the cat pausing and swatting at a butterfly as she waited for us to catch up.

"I have to say, this wasn't a bad idea," Dottie said. "It's the perfect morning for a walk. Skittles gets to have an adventure, and we don't have to worry about her running off and us having to retrieve her."

I smiled. "I thought you might like it."

That all changed when we reached the boardwalk and I turned right instead of left.

"You tricked me," Dottie said, the sheriff's station coming into view. She immediately stopped and refused to take another step.

I held up a finger. "Oh, no. I'm most definitely still planning on getting a breakfast burrito from the diner—I'm starving. I just thought we'd take a little...detour...on the way."

Dottie still refused to move. "We are done interfering, remember? Last time we did this, we ended up walking into the middle of a standoff with a dangerous lunatic."

"That wasn't our fault," I said. "There would have been a standoff with or without our help."

"Yes, but that doesn't mean we need to be there in the thick of things."

I stopped and turned to my sister. "A reporter is bent on proving that our sheriff isn't objective and that outside law enforcement should be brought in. You don't think we should at least warn Sheriff Hart to be careful?"

Dottie hesitated. "Fine. But to be clear, I don't think Juliette has the power to do anything of the sort. Sheriff Hart was elected to oversee the entire county, and he can't be replaced willy nilly."

"No, but social pressure does wonders when you're an elected official."

Dottie continued grumbling but ultimately gestured for me to continue. That was when I noticed two figures standing on the beach. It wasn't unusual for people to be up early around here. The best surfing happened before anyone else was awake, but these weren't two surfers.

I nodded toward the beach. "You recognize them?"

Dottie glanced toward where I was looking. "Not from this distance, I don't. That could be you down there, and I wouldn't know the difference."

Unfortunately, my eyesight wasn't any better. All I could tell was that it was a man and a woman and they were arguing. It got so heated that the woman pushed the man. I was afraid he'd retaliate, but he simply threw his arms in the air and stalked off in the other direction.

"What do you think that was about?" I murmured.

"Nothing to do with us," Dottie said, turning and resuming our walk. She glanced back. "Well, come on. Let's make this quick—you still owe me breakfast."

The angry woman had left, but the man had paused, his gaze following her retreating figure. He then shoved his hands into his pockets and turned his attention to the ocean.

"He looks sad," I said, but reluctantly turned and followed my sister. "It wouldn't hurt to take a second detour."

"And say what?" Dottie asked. "That we had witnessed

their marital dispute and were curious as to the details that had led up to it? When he asks why it's any of our business, we'll have to tell him that it's not. That we're just two nosy old women who had nothing better to do with our time than to bother him."

I opened my mouth to defend myself but realized I had no defense. It was exactly as my sister had said. I was a nosy old woman who liked to know everything about everyone. Especially people I didn't know. Those made the best stories because if I wasn't ever going to see them again, they couldn't get mad at me for telling the neighbors about their troubles.

"Okay," I conceded. "Warning the sheriff is more important anyway."

When we arrived at the sheriff's station, however, he wasn't there. Deputy Randy was, though. He was sitting in a chair, feet propped on the desk in front of him and his eyes closed.

I walked over and tapped him on the shoulder. "Randy, you fell asleep, dear."

My touch startled the deputy so badly that he moved as if to stand up, forgetting that his feet were propped up, and he crashed to the floor.

"I'm so sorry," I said, handing Skittles' leash to Dottie, then rushed forward and offered Randy an arm. "I didn't mean to scare you."

Randy lay on the floor for a moment, his breaths

coming quick as he reoriented himself to his surroundings. "Jo, what time is it?" he asked, his breaths slowing.

I glanced at my watch. "Seven o'clock. We're here to see the sheriff. It's important."

"The sheriff doesn't come in until eight-thirty," Randy said, stifling a yawn and using the desk to pull himself to his feet. "Let me know what you need, and I'll make sure he gets the message."

I smiled and patted his hand. "Thank you. We appreciate it." I paused. "You sure you're all right?"

Randy twisted his neck, earning him a couple of pops. "Much better."

Dottie seemed distracted, and she craned her neck as she looked in the direction of the small jail cell. "Michael Richards finally got tired of singing 'Yellow Submarine,' huh?"

Randy laughed. "Thankfully, yes. If I would have had to listen to that all night, the sheriff may have had another murder on his hands."

Dottie took another step toward the cell, and I turned to the deputy. "You didn't release him early?" I asked. "It would be understandable. No one would blame you, all things considered."

Except the sheriff, of course.

Randy's lips turned down as he glanced toward the cell. "I didn't release him."

I had been afraid of that.

I didn't have my sister's thoughtful approach to situations, and I walked quickly to the cell to get a peek at the renegade surfer.

Only, as I had suspected, it was empty.

I hooked a finger around one of the bars and slowly pulled the door open. A long creak echoed throughout the station. "How long would you say you were asleep?" I asked Randy, turning to him.

His complexion had paled, and he looked like he might pass out.

"Couldn't have been more than a few minutes. Dozed off, that's all." He sounded like he was trying to convince himself, but it wasn't convincing anyone.

"And your keys were exactly where they are now... sitting on the desk next to you?" I asked, raising an eyebrow.

Dottie immediately began reprimanding Deputy Randy about his carelessness, but that was the last thing that poor man needed. He felt bad enough as it was.

I moved to close the cell door, but before I managed it, Skittles took advantage of Dottie's distraction and bolted into the cell, the leash tearing from Dottie's grasp.

"Skittles, now is not the time to play," I scolded. "We'll take you down to the beach after we're done here, I promise."

Skittles paid me no mind. She'd found something to use as a toy and was batting it around. One particularly hard hit sent it skittering clear across the cell.

"Not now. We have an urgent situation on our hands," I told her, and I entered the cell so I could grab her leash.

The moment I stepped through the door, memories of when I'd been locked up in a similar cell washed over me, and my breath hitched. I had pretended the entire experience hadn't affected me—like it had been a humorous experience that, thankfully, had worked out for me in the end.

But I still had nightmares that Dottie and I had never managed to find the real killer. That I had been locked away in prison, no hope of ever getting out.

"You all right, Jo?" Dottie called over.

I squeezed my eyes shut, counted to three, then turned to her and smiled. "Peachy. I think Skittles found a new favorite toy, though." I bent down and squinted. It didn't seem to be a toy at all, and if I wasn't mistaken it was a—

"Is that a strawberry candy like Grandma used to have?" Dottie asked, appearing behind me.

I nodded. "That's what it looks like."

Dottie glanced over to the deputy. "Do you usually give your inmates candy?"

Randy didn't answer right away. He was pacing the office, his expression panicked, likely thinking of what kind of mess he'd be in with the sheriff.

"Deputy Randy," Dottie barked. His gaze snapped to her. "Did this candy belong to Michael Richards? Or did he have any visitors who brought it in with them?"

It took a moment for him to register the question, but

then he slowly shook his head. "I don't think so. But I wasn't here for the entire day. The sheriff needed some things attended to."

It didn't matter that Randy hadn't seen who this candy belonged to. I already knew.

"Lindi Fierce was here," I said, my voice quiet. "That's her candy. She had some on her yesterday morning."

Dottie's gaze whipped back to me. "You're sure?"

I nodded. "Positive. I...borrowed one....from her pocket."

Dottie didn't react to the news that I'd stolen candy off of Bryce's coach, instead beginning to pace the cell. "Lindi was in here," Dottie murmured. "She came in while the deputy was sleeping, saw the keys, and took the opportunity to free Michael." She looked at me. "But why free him when she was Bryce's coach? If there was even a possibility that Michael had killed Bryce, I would think she'd come here to confront him, not—"

"Help him escape," I finished. Yes, I had thought of that. "The surfing community, it must be small. The type of thing where everyone knows everyone else. That's why, even though Isaac hasn't surfed competitively in a long time, he still knows everyone."

"Which means that Lindi likely knows Michael Richards," Dottie said, resuming her pacing. "She might have even coached him at one point."

I sat down on the bed, Dottie's pacing starting to make me dizzy. I glanced over at Deputy Randy's desk but realized I couldn't see it from this angle. Lindi and Michael could have been hidden from view. I searched the walls and ceiling for security cameras but didn't see any.

"Randy," I called from the cell. "Do you have hidden cameras?"

No answer.

I peeked my head out from the cell and saw Randy on the phone on the opposite side of the station. I hoped for his sake that he wasn't speaking with the sheriff. I'd hate to be in his position right now.

Dottie followed me out, picking up Skittles' leash on the way. The cat wasn't happy about losing her newfound freedom, but she grudgingly followed.

I grabbed a tissue from a box on the deputy's desk and then returned to the cell and used the tissue to pick up the candy. I laid it on the deputy's desk and waited for him to finish.

When he did, he was muttering to himself, looking much the worse for wear than he had ten minutes earlier.

"Was that the sheriff?" I asked.

Randy nodded.

"Does he have any idea where Michael Richards might have been headed?"

He shook his head.

I pointed to the piece of candy. "Have the sheriff try Lindi Fierce's room at the bed and breakfast. I have a feeling he'll find your missing fugitive there. And they are going to have a lot to discuss."

13

Randy did as I'd suggested and called the sheriff, telling him the latest development in the missing prisoner dilemma—that Michael had likely been sprung by Lindi Fierce.

Dottie and I sneaked out while he was on the call, because the way the sheriff was shouting, I was pretty sure anyone within a half-mile radius could hear him.

I wiped my hands together, like I was absolving myself of any responsibility of the present situation. "We've pointed the sheriff in the right direction—that's really all we can do at this point, isn't it?"

"Yes, thank goodness," Dottie said. She glanced down at Skittles, who was impatiently pulling her toward the beach. "Sorry, Skittles. We learned our lesson last time we took you to the beach. You have a perfectly good litter box at home that you can use."

"Oh, it wouldn't hurt to let her play around a little bit before heading over to the diner," I said, bending down and scratching Skittles between the ears. "She's been such a good girl and deserves some freedom." It was when I began cooing at the cat and talking baby talk that Dottie pulled on the leash and started walking toward the beach.

"Fine, but only if you promise to not talk like that anymore—there are many reasons I didn't want kids, and that is one of them."

I straightened. "You don't like when I show affection toward Skittles?"

Dottie snorted. "I don't like that it makes a mature adult devolve into—" She waved her hand at me. "This. I mean, honestly, you look ridiculous."

"But she likes it," I protested.

"How do you know babies, or cats in this instance, like to be talked to like that? Maybe they are just as insulted as I am, but they don't have any way of communicating it."

Dottie was about to say more, but her knee gave out on her for a brief second, and she dropped Skittles' leash, using her hand to grab onto me for balance.

"You need to start going to parkour again," I said. "It was really helping before you decided to rage-quit last month."

Skittles rubbed her head against my leg, purring, as Dottie shot me an annoyed look. "I did not 'rage-quit.'" She used air quotes. "I merely decided that Coach David had determined to kill me with those horrendous exercises, and that, just because all of the swooning ladies in our class, who are only there in hopes of dating the coach, put up with it, it didn't mean I needed to as well." She paused. "Where did you learn that phrase, anyway? 'Rage-quit.' It makes you sound like you're trying to be forty years younger than you are. Have you been watching videos on the YouTube again?"

I laughed. "Of course not. That was a one-time thing, and you have to admit, those kittens were pretty darn cute."

Dottie lifted her chin. "I've seen cuter."

"I saw that smile while you were watching. Your face was practically glowing."

My sister liked to pretend she had a heart of iron, but if you could find the right strings to pull, she turned into a pile of fluffy cotton candy. Unfortunately, it also lasted as long as cotton candy did—about thirty seconds.

As Dottie straightened, no longer needing my arm, I noticed that Skittles was no longer with us but had taken advantage of Dottie's loss of balance and was running at full speed toward the beach.

"We have a cat to catch," I said, nodding toward the streak of gray that was weaving between beachgoers.

Dottie released a long sigh. "So much for the leash. Doesn't do much good if I can't hold on to it, does it?" She sounded sad, like it was just another piece of evidence that she was getting old.

"It's not your fault," I said. "Skittles is always looking

for a window of opportunity. Maybe it's time we admit that she's an outside cat."

Dottie walked as quickly as she could in the direction of the beach, limping all the while. "Maybe she is, but I doubt Erwin and the rest of town council will see it like that. He threatened to fine me if he caught Skittles running around town unaccompanied. No one else seems to mind, but he's worried about the safety of the community. Something to do with cleanliness issues. Apparently, he saw her kill a seagull last week. And eat it. Not exactly the kind of thing someone wants to see while lounging on the beach, enjoying their vacation. Of course, Erwin is also the one who complains that he doesn't know what to do about all these seagulls."

"Maybe we could convince him to hire Skittles to take care of the local pests," I suggested, only partially kidding. "But in all seriousness, Dottie, you need to slow down. Skittles will come home when she's good and ready, but if you keep pushing yourself, you may not."

That seemed to strike a nerve, and Dottie increased her speed. "I'm fine, regardless of what Patty has to say. She admitted that the sea air has been good for me, so we're going to leave it at that."

And Dottie said I was the stubborn one.

She eventually stopped, scanning the beach, presumably looking for the cat. It made me wonder if she'd even been chasing Skittles or merely proving that she could.

I stopped beside her, thankful for the rest. I shielded

my eyes, my gaze finally settling on a spot halfway down the beach. "There," I said. "Looks like she's made a friend."

Skittles was lounging next to a couple sitting in beach chairs. The woman was petting her.

"She's socially starved," I told Dottie. "She needs a friend."

"It's safer to keep her in the bakery. She has plenty of room to roam there."

"But she's been so unhappy."

After a long look at Skittles, who looked more content than she had in a long time, Dottie conceded. "Maybe we could get another cat to keep her company, or we can take her on more walks."

I was unsure that would satisfy the tabby, but I let the subject drop, for now. As we approached Skittles, I saw that the woman wore a bikini, her wet hair pulled into a ponytail, but the man she sat with hadn't dressed to swim —he wore slacks and a polo shirt. They appeared to be in deep conversation, his lips pressed together in a firm line.

I stopped, confused, when I realized that I recognized the woman. "That's Lindi Fierce. If she released Michael from prison, though, how can she be here? She wouldn't have had the time."

Looked like the sheriff would be coming up empty-handed. And he'd likely blame Randy for it, poor guy.

"But…" Dottie said, looking equally perplexed. "You're sure she was the one with the strawberry candies?"

I looked up and down the beach, like an alternative

explanation for Lindi's presence would appear. "I'm positive." I nodded toward the pair. "Who is the man with her?"

"No idea."

After one last glance up the beach, I released a heavy sigh. "Well, there's only one way to find out."

Before Dottie could stop me, I walked toward the pair. "Lindi Fierce," I said, approaching. "It's good to see you again. I see that you've met our cat, Skittles."

Annoyance flashed across Lindi's features when she glanced my way, but she quickly covered it with a smile, and she gave me a little wave. "Nice to see you as well." She gestured to the cat. "Beautiful tabby. Friendly, too."

The man who sat with Lindi looked equally annoyed at the interruption, but, unlike Lindi, he didn't try to hide it.

I held out a hand. "Jo Darby. I met your wife yesterday, and she was gracious enough to help me scrape dog poop off the bottom of my shoe. Not many people would be willing to do that for a stranger."

"Lindi and I aren't married. Merely forced acquaintances." He took my outstretched hand. "I'm Victor Pence."

Lindi's lips dipped, but when I looked her way, she forced them back up into a smile. "Victor likes to tease me."

I tried to mask my surprise at discovering Bryce's coach sunbathing with the head judge, but it apparently wasn't very convincing because he smirked. "So, you've heard of me." He leaned back in his chair and rested his hands on his stomach. "How about if we dispense with the awkwardness. Yes, I've heard what people are saying about me, but that's the life of a judge. There are always people who are unhappy with how I'm doing my job, and they would have liked me to be the one who drowned instead of Bryce Carlton. The level of their disdain all depends on which athlete they wanted to win, but I assure you that no one was cheating."

I forced a smile and released the judge's hand. "Except Bryce didn't drown, or haven't you heard?"

I thought back to the conversation I had overheard in the back alleyway. Lindi Fierce knew about the berries, and I'd overheard her saying the name Victor. The judge definitely knew how Bryce had died, so why was he pretending he didn't?

And considering the defensive tone Lindi had adopted on the phone call, Victor Pence thought she'd had something to do with it.

The judge's gaze found the ocean, and his expression morphed into one of neutrality—the type of expression one would use if judging a competition and not wanting others to know who you were secretly rooting for. The man was good—very good—and not someone I'd want to play poker against.

"I've heard conflicting stories," he said. "These reporters that have been stalking us—they all have a different version of what happened, depending on who they've talked to."

Dottie bent over to scratch Skittles behind the ears, and then picked up the leash. "Skittles doesn't normally warm up this quickly," she said in an abrupt change of topic. It made me wonder what she was playing at—she was deliberate in everything she did, especially in situations like this.

"Well, this isn't the first time your cat and I have hung out together on the beach," Lindi said. "Skittles has been out here the last couple of days."

I raised an eyebrow and glanced at Dottie. "So much for keeping her inside. She must have sneaked out, and back in, when we were helping customers. She's a devious one."

Skittles looked up at Dottie, her eyes wide and innocent, and Dottie looked torn, like she didn't want to take Skittles away from her new friends but she also felt we'd overstayed our welcome. That had been why Dottie had changed the subject. She wanted to leave.

Before Dottie had the chance to excuse us, losing us this opportunity to question Lindi and Judge Pence, I jumped in.

"I was really looking forward to the competition this weekend," I said. "Starlight Ridge hasn't hosted anything as big as this, and having you all come here has been very exciting."

Lindi and Victor shared looks, like they were trying to figure out how to get rid of us so they could finish their conversation.

"No disrespect to Bryce Carlton, God rest his soul," I continued. At this point I was just trying to keep the conversation going. "But you know who I would have wanted to win the competition? Other than Isaac, of course."

I knew Dottie didn't want to get any more involved than we were, and for good reason—her health, for one thing. She had been instructed to rest, and the last couple of days had been the opposite of relaxing. But we'd accidentally found Lindi before Sheriff Hart could—my fault, I could admit—and I felt like we needed to take advantage of the situation while we were here. Not only that, but we might have sent the sheriff on a wild goose chase. How could Lindi have both helped Michael Richards' escape and be here on the beach relaxing with Victor Pence?

That was what we needed to find out.

Victor's gaze settled on me—it was intense. "Who?"

I swallowed hard, then said, "Michael Richards."

That garnered the reaction I'd been hoping for.

Lindi choked, probably on her own spit. "Michael? Why on earth would you want him to win? He's a menace to the sport."

"That's why I like him." I fluffed up my pink hair. "As you can see, I'm a bit of a rebel myself. His tattoos and his whole carefree attitude—it's exciting, isn't it?"

Victor's gaze hardened before it softened back to its original neutrality. "Some people certainly share your opinion, but he's a disrupter. And wherever he goes, his uncontrollable fans follow."

"Isn't that the truth," I said. "I mean, bursting into the sheriff's office with that gun, demanding justice for Bryce? Classic."

Dottie's gaze snapped to me, and she leaned in. "Isaac didn't want anyone to know about that," she murmured. "You're playing into Michael's hands—doing exactly what Isaac warned us about."

Yes, I knew. But even if Michael had an ulterior motive for bursting into the sheriff's office and it really had been a publicity stunt, I felt like I could use it to our advantage.

Judge Pence and Lindi looked at me with horror.

"I'm sorry?" Victor said, as if he'd misheard me.

"Oh, yes," I said. "I'm sure the sheriff wanted to keep it under wraps, but it's interesting that, for someone that no one seems to like, he would risk being locked up himself, all to avenge Bryce's death."

Lindi finally found her voice, and her eyebrows dipped in skepticism. "That doesn't sound right. Michael Richards was known for tormenting Bryce any chance he got. In fact, he's the one who started the rumors that Bryce was cheating."

Victor held up a finger. "Which he wasn't, by the way. And he certainly wasn't paying off the judges."

Said the man who had everything to lose if proof ever surfaced that Bryce had been cheating.

"I wonder, though," I said, my words slow. After a

moment of strained silence, I straightened and waved a hand through the air. "I think I read too many novels, and here I am trying to be a real-life detective. That's best left to the professionals, huh?"

Both the judge and Coach Fierce visibly relaxed.

Dottie and I said our goodbyes and pulled a reluctant Skittles away from her new friends.

"We need to talk to Isaac," I whispered as we walked away. "He knows everything about everyone on the surfing scene. Now that we know the questions to ask, I think he could provide some illuminating answers. I don't know if even he realizes how useful he could be."

Dottie frowned. "You promised me breakfast, and then we have a bakery to run, or had you forgotten?"

"Fine, you're right. But as soon as that CLOSED sign is turned, we're paying Isaac a visit." I shook my head. "All this nighttime vigilante business—it's exhausting. I really don't know how Batman does it."

"You've been in bed by nine o'clock every night this week," Dottie said, a smile breaking through.

I gave a solemn nod. "I know. Terrible, isn't it? I'll never be able to keep up this pace."

14

Dottie and I walked the beach just as the sun began to sink, and I pulled in a long breath. There was nothing I loved more than the smell of the ocean. The beach was filled with both locals and tourists, all gathered to see what colors the sunset might have for us this evening. The Sunset Stroll was a Starlight tradition—one of many—and it was one of my favorites, even if I couldn't always stay awake long enough to attend.

I paused when a stray tennis ball rolled my way. I picked it up, but then realized it belonged to Erwin's golden retriever, who was now bounding toward me. I tensed, readying myself for impact. The large dog stopped just in time, but not before spraying me with sand.

"Sorry about that," Erwin said, hurrying over and taking the ball from me. "Donna's been off her game lately. She shouldn't have missed that one."

Erwin was in his late fifties, a bachelor, and the owner of Seaside Bay, a local seafood restaurant. I had never understood how a handsome man like him was still single. Too bad I couldn't ever pursue him, romantically speaking. For one, I had never been interested in that type of thing—romance. And for two, I could only imagine the gossip that would follow us if I dared date a man ten years my junior. From what I understood, that would make me a tiger. Or was it a cougar. Panther? Some kind of big cat—I couldn't remember which.

As a person, though, I liked Erwin. Him, and his dog.

Good thing we hadn't brought Skittles this time. We had arranged to meet Isaac here and, as much as I had enjoyed taking Skittles on her walk earlier that morning, this conversation was going to need our undivided attention.

"No problem," I said. "She's bound to miss one or two."

Erwin gave us a tired smile. "I suppose, but she already barreled over a toddler just before she nearly took you out. It might be time to call it a night."

He then slipped something out of his pocket, unwrapped it, and popped it in his mouth.

A hard candy.

Dottie noticed at the same time I did, and she took a step forward. "Do you mind?" she asked, holding her hand out for the wrapper. "I can throw that away for you."

Erwin's forehead scrunched in confusion, and he

moved to place the wrapper back in his pocket. "You don't need to do that—I'll throw it away when I get home."

"If you don't mind me asking," I said, trying a different approach, "what kind of candy was it? I like to have a candy dish out on the counter for our customers, but I don't think they liked our last batch. It was butterscotch. Seems like it's a dying flavor—the younger people won't touch it."

Erwin's features relaxed, despite his dog prancing around his legs, begging for the ball to be thrown once more. "I do love me a good butterscotch. Unfortunately, it wasn't. It was one of the strawberry ones. I don't think much of it, but you can't complain about free candy, I suppose."

"Free candy?" Dottie asked, unable to hide her piqued interest.

Erwin mistook the meaning behind her question and laughed. "It looks like I've met another sugarholic. I don't know that the walk all the way up the hill to the bed and breakfast is worth it, all for a couple of pieces of hard candy. It really isn't that great."

My gaze whipped to Dottie. "Anyone staying at the bed and breakfast had access to that candy."

She nodded to Erwin. "Or anyone who happened to be passing through."

Well, darn. That just expanded our suspect pool by quite a bit. The sheriff wasn't going to be happy with

Dottie and me, sending him all the way up to Lindi's room for nothing.

It wasn't long after Erwin and his golden retriever had left us that Isaac appeared from behind one of the many bonfires that dotted the shoreline. His gaze darted first one way, then the other, as if he was on high alert. It eventually landed on us, and he casually walked over, his hands shoved in his pockets. "You two aren't easy to find. You really should consider cellphones—been here for twenty minutes now."

"Sorry, Isaac," I said. "It's something that Dottie and I have been considering. Our lives have been very busy of late, and we don't stay at home nearly as much as we used to."

His gaze jumped again, this time to something behind me. "If it's all the same to you, I think I'd like to move this conversation back to your bakery. I didn't realize there were so many spectators who have stuck around."

"Spectators...or reporters?" Dottie asked, nodding to a man standing not far from us. His camera was aimed in our direction.

Isaac bent his head low. "Would you two ladies give me the honor of escorting you home? It's getting dark."

I glanced at my watch. It was impossible to tell the time with the limited light, but I said, "Oh I didn't realize it was so late. We have to get an early start at the bakery, you know."

"Always working too hard," Isaac said, and we left the

beach, arm in arm. I glanced back to see if anyone bothered to follow us, but the reporter merely watched, his camera still trained on Isaac.

Once I thought we were at a safe enough distance, I pulled my arm from Isaac's. "Something weird is going on with this investigation, Isaac, and I'm afraid that we need your help."

"I don't know how much help I can be," he said. "My strategy right now is to lie low and not attract attention until the sheriff works things out. I'm sure he has it under control." His voice lacked conviction.

Dottie nodded. "That's what I said."

"He doesn't know these surfers like you do," I said, exasperated. "I want to support Sheriff Hart as much as the next person, but the fact is that he doesn't understand the dynamics any more than I do." I glanced at Isaac. "Did you hear that someone broke Michael Richards out of jail? And I have it on good authority that it was someone who is staying at the bed and breakfast."

"Or merely stopped by to visit," Dottie added.

I nodded in concession. "And that's not to mention that Felicity, his girlfriend, has been oddly absent, all things considered, and Bryce's former coach and the head judge seem at odds with one another. Of course, they might always be like that, but I still think it's—"

Isaac held up a finger. "I'm sorry, but Michael has gone missing?"

"Guess Randy managed to do one thing right and keep

things quiet," Dottie mumbled as we reached the bakery's front doors.

"He means well," I said, then turned to Isaac. "Yes. Someone broke Michael out while Deputy Randy was sleeping. They left something behind, though. A clue."

Dottie snorted. "A clue that all of Starlight Ridge had access to."

I held in an eye roll as we all paraded inside, then motioned for Isaac to have a seat at the display counter. "I'll go rustle us up some dessert. In the meantime, do you know of anyone in your surfing gang who might do something like break Michael out of jail? I assume it takes a certain type of person. They were very brazen, for one, stealing the deputy's keys like that."

Isaac looked like he was fighting a smile. "I don't really have a...gang...anymore, and Michael prides himself on being a lone wolf. There are his fans, of course. And..." He trailed off, his face taking on a distant expression, like he was thinking of something but deciding whether he should say it aloud.

"Macaron for your thoughts," I said.

Isaac's gaze returned to me. "I doubt she'd do something like this. It was always harmless flirting. Nothing more."

"Who?" Dottie asked.

"Felicity," I guessed. "I noticed it on the morning of the competition."

Isaac allowed himself to smile this time. "Some things

never change, I guess. No matter how long I'm away from the scene. Love triangles have always been a constant source of trouble for surfers."

"Just another reason that surfing is bad for your health," I said with a solemn nod.

Dottie looked at Isaac. "You're saying that Felicity was in a love triangle and that Bryce was the only thing standing in the way of her and Michael getting together."

He raised a shoulder. "I guess. But like I said, Michael is a lone wolf, and even though he has a fun time flirting with...well...everyone, I doubt he's looking for anything serious. And to kill Bryce for something like that?" He shook his head. "I don't think so."

"Maybe he's tired of being alone. Or maybe the only reason he's alone is because he doesn't have Felicity. People have killed for a lot less," I said. "Regardless, I'm going to get those macarons I promised you, and maybe a slice of bread pudding to go along with it. We're going to need some sugar to help us figure all this out."

By the time I returned, Dottie and Isaac were discussing other possible suspects.

"We've met a reporter who is a megafan of Bryce's," she was saying. "She's a bit intense—if she believed that Michael was exacting justice on Bryce's behalf, she could have freed him. And she'd have the bonus of an exclusive interview that the other reporters would kill for."

We all grimaced.

"I know," she said. "I heard it as soon as I said it."

I had filled one of the bakery's boxes with a variety of macarons and a couple of slices of bread pudding, and I placed it on the counter for us to all share. I started with a lemon macaron.

"What do you know about Lindi Fierce?" I asked Isaac, crumbs falling from my lips as I talked. I paused to wipe them with a tissue from my pocket. "She and that judge, Victor Pence, seemed like something weird was going on between them at the beach today."

Isaac didn't look the least bit fazed and raised a shoulder. "When we're all done for the day, it's not unusual to end up relaxing at the same bars or restaurants. Coach Fierce and Judge Pence have been known to be friendly when things have gone well for Bryce. When things haven't gone so well, it's not unusual for coaches to be angry with the judges."

"Any physical altercations?" I asked, thinking of the arguing couple on the beach earlier. It could have been them.

Isaac looked between Dottie and me, and then said, his words slow, "Emotions run high during a competition. Nothing that a drink and some karaoke can't fix."

Dottie rested a hand on Isaac's. "You said you thought Bryce was paying off the judges," she kindly reminded him. "And you aren't the only one who thinks that. Could Lindi and Victor Pence have had some sort of arrangement?"

Isaac hesitated, carefully choosing his words. "There

were rumors that Bryce was paying off the judges, but that's all they were. Rumors."

"You're having second thoughts about that theory," Dottie said.

Isaac nodded. "Being involved in an accident like he was—I've thought of nothing but Bryce and his death since it happened. I know I swore up and down that Bryce didn't deserve the scores he got, but the more I think about it, the more I don't think he would have cheated. He had too much pride for something like that."

"Being with someone in their last moments has an impact, doesn't it?" I said, offering him a slice of the bread pudding. "We start seeing them in a better light—a kinder one."

Isaac took the slice of pudding from me and placed it on a napkin in front of him. "He didn't mean to cut me off," he said. "At first I thought he was deliberately sabotaging me, and I was so angry. But then I saw the look on his face as he doubled over." He shook his head. "I spent so much time seeing Bryce as my rival that anytime I thought I'd been judged unfairly, I blamed him. It had to be his fault. Eventually, I thought, what was the point?"

"Is that why you stepped away from competing?" Dottie asked.

Isaac's gaze landed on the front windows. It was dark now. "It was at a time when it felt like my whole life was falling apart around me. I no longer had a safe place to land. I thought that if I stopped competing—only surfed for me—that things would get better."

I smiled and offered him a plastic fork for his bread pudding. "It rarely does—not until you face things head on."

We fell silent for a few minutes, lost in our own thoughts. Maybe thinking about all the times we had run from a situation and regretted it. The only sounds were of us nibbling on the pastries in front of us.

It got to be too much, and I cleared my throat. "We can speculate all day long who might have killed Bryce and who might have freed Michael. It could be the same person—probably isn't. But speculation isn't going to solve anything. Not without evidence." I looked at Isaac. "You know these people better than anyone investigating Bryce's murder. But it was unfair for us to ask you here tonight. You've been through a terrible trauma, and I never wanted to guilt you into a position you didn't want to be in."

Isaac's gaze dropped, and he played with his bread pudding. He still hadn't tried it. I tried not to be offended and instead focus on what mattered.

"People think I did it," he said, his voice soft. "And I don't blame them. I was always vocal in my criticism of Bryce and his talents—or lack thereof." He caught himself and gave us a sheepish smile. "It's a hard habit to break, even now." His gaze rose. "I want to help, in any way I can."

I looked at Dottie. I didn't think she'd try to stop us—

she'd likely given that up long ago—but that didn't mean she was with us.

She studied me for a moment before turning to Isaac. "I don't suppose the Warners have security cameras set up at the bed and breakfast, do they? We could watch the footage and see how many people took a strawberry candy from the front desk. That would at least give us a starting place."

I doubted the bed and breakfast would have anything that high tech, but then I saw the hesitation on Isaac's face.

"What?" Dottie asked him, noticing it too.

Isaac was quiet, probably already regretting saying he'd help us in our investigation.

"They do have a camera," I guessed. "But you don't want us to see what's on it."

After another hesitation, Isaac said, "It's not that. I mean, yes, they do have a camera. Got it a couple of years ago when they had some vandalism from rowdy tourists. But—" He blew out a hard breath and ran a hand through his hair. "You're more than welcome to ask if you can look at the footage, but I'm afraid I can't go with you. I'm not exactly welcome there."

15

Dottie's brows creased, and she studied Isaac. She was starting to go into cop mode. That was good for us, but bad for Isaac.

"Why don't they want you there?" she asked. "What did you do?"

Isaac's full focus was now on the bread pudding in front of him, and he was mutilating it with his fork. Seriously, if he didn't want it, he could have just told me.

He glanced up, blinking a couple of times as he tried to hide the moisture that had pooled in his eyes. "It's awkward when the woman you were going to marry runs off to Hollywood and never returns, but you still live in the same small town as her family. I haven't talked to them in a couple of years. They've reached out, but I've never returned their calls or texts. Couldn't bring myself to. They run the bed and breakfast, so it's been fairly easy to avoid them. It's not like they own the surf shop or something like that. But I think that me speaking to them for the first time since their daughter left—after all this time—well, asking to see their security cameras is going to be a strange request. And potentially offensive."

I'd say so.

Dottie released a hard breath. "When you said your life had fallen apart, you weren't kidding."

Isaac set down his fork. "When Leanne left, I blamed myself for everything, and my depression spiraled out of control. I couldn't stop wondering if I was the reason she felt she needed more. Maybe I was gone too often, competing. Maybe she felt like I hadn't given her the attention she'd needed, or that I didn't care."

"That's the real reason you stopped competing," I said softly.

He nodded. "So that I would be here if she ever returned. So that she could see I was trying."

"You don't need to come with us," Dottie said. "You go home and lie low. The less ammunition these reporters have, the better. We can take care of things from here."

Isaac started to nod, but it morphed into a shake of his head. "No. I said I was going to help, and I will. If that means facing Leanne's parents, so be it."

Talk about drama. I had learned more about Isaac and his surfing world in the past thirty minutes than I had since Dottie and I had first moved to town. I loved

Starlight Ridge, but it made me wonder if I would have loved it so much if I had grown up here. I would certainly have hated for my "issue" to be common knowledge among everyone I came in contact with—everyone hugging their purses a little tighter, wondering if they would be my next victim.

"All right," Dottie said with a quick nod. "It's getting a bit late now, so we'll go to the bed and breakfast in the morning. Meet us here, and I'll drive." She held up a finger. "But remember why we're there. We don't have time for tears and reconciliation. Not when a murderer is on the loose, and every day that passes lessens our chances of discovering the truth. Otherwise—"

"The sheriff will come right back for me," Isaac said, his entire body drooping. He sounded miserable at the prospect, and I couldn't help but feel so sorry for him.

I rested a hand on his arm until his gaze rose and met mine. "We won't let that happen," I told him kindly.

He smiled, but it lacked conviction, and he turned to leave. "See you in the morning, then. Nine o'clock?"

"Make it eight-thirty," Dottie said. "We need to be done before the bakery opens at ten."

IT TOOK a long time for eight-thirty to come around. I hadn't been able to sleep and was up and ready to go by six o'clock. Dottie was up even before I was.

"Now what?" I asked, drumming my fingers on the

small dining room table, an empty bowl of Cream of Wheat sitting in front of me.

"We wait," Dottie said. "Or see if Autumn needs help in the kitchen downstairs. I heard her come in about half an hour ago."

I snorted. "Right. You know she'll never let us into the inner sanctum. She says we just get in the way—we throw her off her groove."

Dottie smiled. "It's true, we do get in the way."

Silence fell over us, and Dottie's smile disappeared.

"I could start getting Skittles ready," I said.

She raised an eyebrow. "You're not really thinking about bringing her with us, are you? She'll be a distraction."

"Skittles needs fresh air and exercise, and once we return, we won't have time to take her outside," I said. "You know how crazy she gets when she's cooped up all day."

Dottie didn't respond. If I hadn't already been looking at her, I wouldn't have even noticed the barely perceptible nod.

"Do you think we're just wasting our time, running around town like this?" I asked, attempting a change of subject. Talking to Dottie this morning was like trying to talk to an iron statue. "If Michael Richards did kill Bryce, he's likely long gone by now. He wouldn't stick around."

"The sheriff asked all athletes, coaches, and judges to stay in town until he could clear them," Dottie said.

I laughed. "Somehow I doubt that a murderer is interested in keeping to the rules. Besides, the sheriff can't keep everyone here indefinitely. They are all scheduled to head back home tomorrow."

"And I doubt they'll stay a minute longer. Puts the sheriff in a bit of a time crunch, doesn't it?" Dottie said.

I nodded. "If the murderer really was Felicity, like the sheriff initially thought, he'd have arrested her by now. Probably means he doesn't have enough evidence."

A pause.

"Yup."

More silence.

I tilted my head to the side. "Not very talkative this morning."

Dottie avoided my gaze. "That's not so unusual for me."

No, it wasn't. But there was something about the way she was sitting there, quiet, not looking at me, that made me think this was more than just her usual early morning tiredness.

"If you're not feeling up to going to the bed and breakfast—" I started.

Dottie immediately pushed her chair away from the table and stood. "I'm fine." And then she moved to the staircase to prove it. "I'll check in with Autumn and meet you downstairs. If you're wanting to bring Skittles to the bed and breakfast with us, now's the time to put on her harness. She's just tired enough that she probably won't put up much of a fight."

I watched my sister for another moment, wondering

what was actually going on with her, but decided not to push it.

It took some doing, but I managed to get the cat's harness on just before Isaac knocked on our back door.

"Think Becky Warner will let us actually look at the surveillance videos?" I called to Dottie as I made my way down the stairs, Skittles attempting to pull me faster than I could go.

"She'll let Isaac," Dottie said, sounding far more confident than I felt. "He loves her daughter, remember? As awkward as it will be for him, I doubt Becky would consider saying no."

I hoped she was right, or this was going to be awkward for all of us.

THE BED and breakfast was a beautiful home with a wraparound porch and a serenity garden in the back. The perfect place for a relaxing getaway.

And yet, none of us could bring ourselves to walk through that front door.

The three of us stood in front of the bed and breakfast, looking at the door as if it were going to attack us. Skittles became impatient and pulled on the leash, begging to explore.

"It's still early," I said. "Think the Warners will be up?"

No one answered me.

"I haven't been up here since Leanne left," Isaac said after a long moment, his voice soft.

More silence.

"Oh, this is ridiculous," Dottie said, stepping forward. "The worst that can happen is that they say we can't look at the videos and then we all go to the diner for breakfast." She placed a hand on the doorknob.

"It is a bit of an invasion of privacy, isn't it?" I said. "I've never looked at a security video before. It feels like spying."

Dottie turned her head, her hand still on the door-knob. "That's exactly what it is. But we need a list of every person who took one of those strawberry candies. It will help narrow things down for the sheriff. Maybe it won't prove who killed Bryce, but discovering who broke Michael out of jail is a step in the right direction. Some-times, the—"

Dottie was prevented from saying more when the front door flew open, with Dottie still attached to it. Startled, Skittles leaped forward, straining against the leash. When that escape attempt failed, she ran in circles, wrapping the leash around my ankles.

"Oh my," Becky Warner said, catching Dottie before she could fall through the open doorway. "I'm so sorry. You three have been standing on this porch for the past ten minutes, and I figured if you weren't going to enter, I might as well be the one to let you in."

I gave her an embarrassed smile as I attempted to

unwind myself from the leash, all while Skittles was trying to run inside.

"Thank you, Becky," I started. "You see, it's the funniest thing..." And then I stopped, because I had no idea what the funniest thing was. Nothing about the reason we were there was remotely humorous.

Dottie brushed herself off, straightened, and opened her mouth to speak, but when nothing came out, Becky merely laughed and shook her head.

"Come into the dining room and have some fruit and Jessie's lemon tarts." She glanced at the cat. "I think I could even rustle up some tuna fish or chicken for the carnivore of the group."

"Thank you," I said. "Skittles appreciates the hospitality."

Becky nodded her acknowledgement and pulled the door open wider for us to enter. "I'm especially happy to see you, young man," she said as Isaac passed her. "It's been a long time coming."

Isaac's gaze dropped, and he mumbled, "Yes, ma'am."

We were shuffled through the entryway and then past the check-in desk. I noted the dish of strawberry hard candies that sat on the desk. It was only half full.

"Your candy dish is sure popular," I said. "It's a nice touch for when people first arrive."

Becky glanced at the desk before leading us into the dining room. "You'd think so, but I've had that strawberry candy for nearly a year now—no one will touch it. I finally got a guest who loves the stuff. Thank goodness—I might finally be able to buy some new candy."

Dottie and I exchanged surprised looks. If only one guest was eating those candies, then it really had been Lindi Fierce who had broken Michael out of jail.

"I'll be right back with your breakfast," Becky said with a warm smile. "Sit wherever you like." She then walked to a long table on the opposite side of the room. It was filled with fruit and pastries, and I was suddenly hungry again, my previous breakfast of Cream of Wheat a distant memory.

"I know what you're thinking," Dottie said, slipping into a chair at a nearby table. "But just because Lindi had one in her pocket doesn't mean she is the one who has been eating all of them. It may have been offered to her and she took it to be polite."

"She's a well-regarded coach," I said, settling in next to my sister and holding Skittles' leash, keeping her from wandering too far. I doubted the other guests would appreciate a cat leaping onto their table and into their food—that was Skittles' signature move. "Lindi didn't get where she is by being polite."

We quieted when Becky returned with our plates of food. She set a small bowl of tuna on the floor, and Skittles dashed toward it like she hadn't eaten for weeks. "Don't get used to having tuna for breakfast," I told her. "That's what fancy cats eat. Dry food is good enough for us."

I glanced around at the other tables, noting that most

of the surfing competitors were here. Michael Richards was, of course, missing. But I recognized many of the others, including Felicity, who sat in a corner along with...

"Lindi Fierce," I whispered to Dottie. "Far right corner."

I had known that the coaches and athletes were staying in the bed and breakfast, but I hadn't pieced together that when we showed up, they'd all be here. I figured they'd be out on the town, getting in some early morning surfing, or sleeping in on their last day in Starlight Ridge.

"The sheriff asked that no one go out surfing while Bryce's death is still an active investigation," Becky murmured, noting where my gaze had landed. "Doesn't want to risk the murderer striking again. Breakfast's been a bit crowded ever since."

She paused.

"I love seeing all three of you," she said, her gaze resting on Isaac. Her attention then returned to Dottie and me. "But I have to say that I'm surprised. It doesn't seem like you're here just for Jessie's lemon tarts."

Dottie and I exchanged glances, silently asking if now was the right time to tell Becky our true intentions.

"You need something," Becky guessed, looking to Isaac for confirmation.

He nodded. "We have reason to believe that a clue to catching Bryce's murderer could lie on your security camera footage. We wondered if we might take a look." He gestured to his plate. "After finishing this delicious breakfast, of course. No rush."

Becky studied the three of us, likely wondering how we'd all ended up involved in this. "You're not doing this on behalf of the sheriff," she finally said. "It's probably best that you don't get yourselves involved." She looked at Dottie. "I expected better from you."

Dottie opened her mouth to respond, but nothing came out.

"Now, wait just a moment there," I said. "How do you know that we aren't here on strict instructions from the sheriff? He's a very busy man, you know. Practically a one-man band."

Becky folded her arms over her chest. "Because he's already been here, and he's looked at our cameras."

I should have known that would have been one of the first things he'd have done, looking to see if there was anything suspicious on the security footage. Most people with motive to harm the surfer were staying here, and I would have been disappointed in him if he hadn't. But the sheriff hadn't been looking for strawberry candies.

Isaac spoke up, his voice quiet. "Please, Mrs. Warner. We won't take long. It's just—if the sheriff doesn't find what he's looking for by tomorrow, I'm the most obvious suspect. Aside from Michael Richards, I suppose, now that he's gone missing." He then looked her straight in the eyes. "Please. Just this once."

She hesitated, her gaze taking in the room of athletes

and coaches enjoying their breakfast, oblivious to the conversation occurring here.

"Fine," Becky said, turning back to Isaac. "If you think it will help. Before you do, though, I've been wanting to talk to you." Isaac looked like he was about to protest, but she held up a hand, stopping him. "I want you to know that Mr. Warner and myself—we're on your side. It's not fair what Leanne did to you, disappearing like that. And I'm sorry for what you've had to go through. If it's any consolation, she doesn't call us anymore either. And if there is—"

Isaac stood, pushing his plate away. "Thank you, but it's fine. I've moved on." His tone was crisp but polite. "You okay if I go ahead and look at that footage now?"

Becky seemed taken aback by his abrupt change of tone, but she stepped back and gestured toward another part of the building. "Go right ahead. It's the least I can do for you, all things considered."

I looked at my plate, still full of food, torn between following Isaac and staying to finish eating.

"Leave it," Dottie murmured, standing.

Maybe Isaac didn't feel the need to eat—wanted to get the job done as quickly as possible. That didn't mean I had to.

"You two go ahead," I said. "This lemon tart and I have some unfinished business. Besides, Skittles isn't quite done yet." Dottie raised an eyebrow, and I saw that Skittles had eaten every last bit of tuna and was now merely licking an empty bowl, trying to get what juice she could. I shooed Dottie away with my hand. "Honestly, we'll be along shortly."

Dottie eyed me like she thought I was up to something but then raised a shoulder. "If you say so." She followed Isaac out.

My sister had every right to be suspicious, because this tart wasn't the only unfinished business I had in here, and I hoped Skittles would play along.

16

I tried to look nonchalant, bending down and petting Skittles between taking bites of my food. I wasn't yet sure how I wanted to play this.

This was probably a waste of time, but Felicity and Lindi Fierce must have some sort of relationship, considering how many hours Bryce had spent training with his coach. It was likely that Felicity had joined him on many of these occasions. If I had grown up in Kentucky and was now dating a competitive surfer, I would try to learn everything I could about the sport. I'd probably even try to learn the sport myself, and a lot can be learned from watching.

Which was why I didn't approach the two women. Not yet. I was here to watch.

These were two women who were familiar with each other but not necessarily friendly. Neither smiled as they ate. Felicity almost seemed bored. They certainly didn't

seem like they were co-conspirators in a plot to rid themselves of a man who had given them both grief.

It was interesting, though, that his death had benefited
them both—Felicity with her not-so-secret attraction to
Michael Richards and accusations against Bryce potentially harming Lindi's career. If it was proved that he'd
been cheating, I doubted Lindi would find another surfer
who would work with her.

Skittles meowed, her tuna fish juice completely gone,
and I smiled down at her. "All right. We can go."

When I glanced up, both Lindi and Felicity were
looking at me, Skittles' meow alerting them to my presence. I smiled and waved, then pushed myself up from the
table.

"What a pleasant surprise," I said, walking over to
where they were seated. "I hadn't expected to see you two
lovely ladies here. In all honesty, I'd forgotten that this was
where the surfing tournament had arranged for athletes to
stay."

Lindi returned a forced smile. "Do you come here for
breakfast often?"

"Not as often as I'd like," I said, then lowered my voice
to a conspiratorial whisper. "It's Skittles, you see. She has
terrible manners when she eats out in public, and it's
embarrassing. I appreciate that Mrs. Warner treats her so
well, with her fancy tuna fish and all that, but Dottie and I
have a reputation to uphold, you know."

Felicity stifled a laugh. "Yes, I completely understand. I

feel the same way about my own cat. Can't take her anywhere."

I gave a solemn nod. "It's why we had to buy this harness. She hates it, the poor thing, but it's the only way we can go out in public nowadays." I pulled out a chair from their table and turned to Lindi. "Do you mind?" I didn't wait for an answer and plunked myself down. "She really is a wonderful cat. I don't know if you heard, but just a few months ago, Skittles ran into one of our neighbors' homes—the cat went absolutely bonkers—and while in there, she found the murder weapon that had been used to kill a local woman."

Felicity gasped, and her eyes widened. "You're kidding."

My gaze didn't leave Lindi. "I'm not. And then, just a couple of days ago, Skittles found a vital clue in the jail cell that Michael Richards had escaped from. It's like she's drawn to these things—like she's a reincarnated Sherlock Holmes. But that's hardly safe, is it? Can't have her running all over town, digging up guns and knives and all that."

"She found a gun?" Felicity asked, her voice half-hoarse.

I glanced at her. "Oh no, not at all. Poison."

Lindi was watching me, her gaze scrutinizing. "You think this clue Skittles found in Michael's jail cell is important, then?"

I nodded. "It's going to lead us to Bryce's killer, I'm sure of it."

"An amazing cat," Lindi said, her words slow. "If I were you, I wouldn't let her out of your sight. Who knows what she'll discover next."

It may have been my imagination, but I could have sworn a threat lay somewhere in there.

"We try not to," I said, "but she's a slippery thing. Sneaks out between customers, as you know. She's visited you on the beach on more than one occasion."

Lindi folded her napkin and placed it on her empty plate. "Yes, she seems to have a mind of her own. That being said, it's not entirely appropriate to bring pets into the dining room of a restaurant, is it? Pet dander and all that."

"No, I suppose not," I said, pushing my chair back from the table. I moved to stand but changed my mind at the last second. I looked at Felicity. "I've been thinking about you. Everything that's happened over the past few days— it's just awful. Will you be all right, now that you've lost two people you cared for?"

Felicity gave me a quizzical look. "Two people?"

"Yes, Bryce Carlton and now Michael Richards. I hear he's missing, and I do hope he's okay."

Felicity studied me, her expression now guarded and her gaze curious. "I think I've underestimated you."

I smiled. "Most do, dear. It's the curse of the elderly— people think just 'cause we're old that we've gone mad."

"I don't think you're mad," Felicity said, her words slow. "But I do think you're nosy."

That made me laugh, because it was true. I liked that Felicity had no problem calling me out on it. "Right you are. Another curse of the elderly. We don't know how to mind our own damn business."

Lindi was quiet while watching the exchange, and she seemed annoyed. "How did you know about Felicity and Michael? I've had to work hard to keep that one under wraps. It wouldn't do any good for Bryce's or Michael's reputation."

"Did Michael know he was supposed to be keeping things under wraps?" I asked, turning to Lindi. "He openly flirted with Felicity just before the competition, and right in front of me, no less." Not to mention that Isaac knew. That likely meant every competitor out there had also been in the know.

"That's the evidence you were going on?" Lindi released a disbelieving laugh. "Michael flirted with everyone—that was how I was able to keep it quiet."

I scrunched up my eyebrows, pretending to be perplexed by the whole situation. "It seemed so genuine."

Lindi shook her head. "I shouldn't have said anything. I trust you'll be able to keep this to yourself."

I was unsure what it was Lindi wanted me to keep to myself. If I was understanding her correctly, this meant Felicity and Michael had a more serious relationship than I'd realized and what I'd witnessed hadn't been harmless flirting. It had been an act to cover up what was really going on between the two of them.

I had to think on that a moment. I didn't want to lie to Lindi, but I was certainly going to be sharing this entire exchange with Dottie and Isaac. No promise was going to stop that from happening.

Before I could piece together how I would respond, Felicity turned to Lindi. "Why does it matter now that Bryce is dead?"

Lindi's lips dipped into a frown. "And how would it look if Bryce's girlfriend is seen with his rival mere days after his death? People would think you might have had something to do with it."

"It's normal for people to move on quickly. Men do it all the time," Felicity said, sticking her chin out.

They talked as if they knew where Michael was. As if he'd reappear any moment and he and Felicity would be a happy couple without a care in the world. They certainly weren't worried about the sheriff.

"I shouldn't keep you any longer than I have," I said, pulling on Skittles' leash. She had gotten bored and was half-asleep under the table. She opened one eye, annoyed at being woken, then promptly closed it again. "It's nice that you two can still be friendly, even with everything that's happened."

Lindi and Felicity shared looks that made me think I was missing something, but I was having trouble deciphering what it could be.

My gaze moved from Felicity's questioning eyes to Lindi's pursed lips. Back to Felicity's eyes. They were gray.

Not many people had gray eyes. Only about three percent of the population—I had learned that from the YouTube. Dottie could say what she liked about it, but all those random videos I'd stayed up late watching had paid off, because I had just noticed Lindi's eye color. Also gray.

"Sisters," I whispered.

Felicity's eyebrows popped up in surprise. "What did you say?"

My heart nearly stopped from shock. The world quieted around me, then it spun, and I had to sink back into my chair to keep myself from falling. How had they managed to keep it a secret? I hadn't had a clue they were related. Not even an inkling that this was a possibility.

Of course, they had different last names. Lindi had probably changed hers for professional reasons, just like the reporter, Juliette Bigsby, had done. I would have done the same thing if I were Lindi—Fierce was a wonderful last name for a surfing coach. Lindi Andrews didn't quite have the same ring to it.

Lindi's gaze snapped to her sister. "Who else have you told?"

Felicity's face had paled by three shades, and her gaze jumped between me and her sister. "I haven't told anyone, I swear."

"Well, somehow the old lady knows, and who knows how many other people."

Felicity pulled in a long breath in what seemed like a

self-calming technique. "So what? We're sisters. It's not like that will affect anything."

"No, but that is why she agreed to coach Bryce in the first place," I guessed. "Because he was your boyfriend and you asked her to. She'd rather have coached Isaac, but you convinced her to take a chance on Bryce Carlton."

"And it paid off too," Felicity snapped, all patience and decorum gone. Her eyes narrowed in anger. "Coaching Bryce was the best thing that ever happened to her—took her career to a whole new level."

I didn't allow Felicity's anger to rattle me. "Then why does she regret it?"

It was Lindi's turn to be angry. It seemed Felicity hadn't been the only one who had told me more than she should have, and I'd always been terrible at keeping secrets. Especially when I didn't know it had been one.

Lindi pushed back her chair and stood. "I think it's time you leave, Mrs..."

She'd evidently forgotten my name.

"Jo," I said with a smile. "I do have places I need to be, so thank you for the reminder." I nodded to a backpack sitting on the chair next to her. "And it looks like you do too. Hiking?"

"Yes. Up to Starlight Ridge," Lindi said, her fierce gaze unnerving.

"That's a wonderful hike this time of year," I said. "Just one last thing." I reached into my pocket and pulled out a strawberry hard candy that I'd taken from the dish up front. "I adore these candies that Mrs. Warner puts out for the guests, and I grabbed a few too many. Would either of you like one?"

There wasn't a friendly face between them, both women eyeing me skeptically.

"I don't like sugar," Lindi said, even as Felicity had begun to reach for the offered treat. Her hand immediately retracted.

"Neither do I," Felicity said.

I didn't let my smile dip. "No worries. It only means more for me later." I glanced down at the sleeping cat. "Come along, Skittles. You've had your treat and your nap. It's time we get home to open the bakery."

I waved a friendly goodbye to Lindi and Felicity, but Skittles still refused to budge, so I had to lift her into my arms and carry her out.

As I left, I wondered if Sheriff Hart knew of this new revelation. I couldn't help but hope that I would be the one to deliver the good news—I'd always had a certain pride about knowing things that others didn't.

17

S tairs. My nemesis.

And there were so many of them. My gaze followed the winding staircase that led to the second floor, my heart already racing from the exertion I hadn't yet put myself through.

I was sure the Warners kept their security feed on the main floor, probably in the back where their offices were, and I'd eventually make my way to where Isaac and Dottie were. But right now I was more interested in what was upstairs. Sheriff Hart would have already checked Lindi's room for evidence that Michael Richards was hidden there, but I doubted he'd checked Felicity's.

"Can I help you with anything, Jo?" Becky asked, entering the lobby and stepping behind the desk. She lowered her voice. "Isaac and Dottie are still looking through the security feed. Would you like me to show you where they are?"

I hesitated and glanced toward the dining room. "Actually, I was hoping to visit Bryce Carlton's girlfriend, Felicity. We've become good friends over the past few days, but she didn't answer when I knocked on her door. I wondered if she had an adjoining room with Bryce. She could be in his room—everyone deals with grief differently. Honestly, that's why Dottie and I bought our bakery. We wanted to feel close to our sister after she passed away. Maybe Felicity is the same way and she wanted to feel close to Bryce."

I hated lying to Becky, but I couldn't come right out and ask if Felicity had an adjoining room with Lindi Fierce, who was not only Bryce's coach but also Felicity's sister. That could be an easy way to hide Michael—move him between the two rooms, depending on which one was being searched.

Becky gave me a hospitable smile, like she knew I was lying through my teeth but wasn't going to call me out on it. She'd have known that Felicity was in the dining room with the other guests, but Becky had likely needed to get very good at polite decorum long ago, dealing with a wide range of guests on a daily basis.

"No, I'm sorry," she said. "We don't have adjoining rooms at our bed and breakfast—we're not quite fancy enough for something like that."

I returned her smile. "Oh, well, it's possible I remembered her room number wrong—I'm always mixing up my numbers. Would you mind writing it down for me? If I ask you to tell it to me, I'll just forget again by the time I get to the top of the stairs." I looked up to where they wound toward the second floor and found myself once again short of breath.

Becky didn't even pretend to believe me this time, but that didn't stop her from writing down the number. "I shouldn't be doing this, you know."

"It's not like you're giving me the key," I said. "Unless—"

Becky's eyes seemed to laugh at me as she quickly said, "No. Just the room number."

I took the small piece of paper from her before she could change her mind. "Thank you. I do appreciate it. It's all for the greater good, you know."

By the time I reached the top of the stairs, I was fairly certain my guardian angels were on their way to take me home. The human heart wasn't meant to beat the way mine was. If Dottie were here, she'd ask if I was certain it would be Heaven I was headed to. Maybe the angels escorting me wouldn't have halos but pitchforks instead.

And then I would laugh at her, because, although I hadn't been perfect in life, I'd hardly been terrible enough to end up surrounded by fire and brimstone. I doubted God cared very much about my propensity for stealing; it wasn't like I meant to. As for all my other faults—well, there were people who'd done far worse.

I hadn't been able to carry Skittles at the same time I'd climbed the stairs, and she'd had to be prodded the entire way up. She looked up at me grumpily. For her, that staircase might as well have been Mount Everest.

"The exercise is good for you," I said, then pulled the crumpled piece of paper that had Felicity's room number on it from my pocket.

203.

I turned to the left and saw that I was at 215.

More walking. Nearly all the way to the end of the hallway, it turned out.

Not great for me or Skittles, but lucky for someone that wanted to hide a fugitive from the law. They'd have plenty of warning that someone was coming.

By the time I reached 203, I needed to take another breathing break. It was fortunate that Lindi and Felicity were going hiking, giving me plenty of time.

After my heart rate had slowed enough that I could speak without gasping, I knocked on Felicity's door and stepped to the side so I wouldn't be seen through the peephole. I'd learned that tactic from...oh, that one movie. I couldn't remember the name. I did know it had that actor I liked, though. Dark hair, handsome face. I'd watch anything he was in, regardless of the reviews.

The funny thing was, even after all this planning and getting myself and Skittles up that flight of stairs, I hadn't actually expected to find Michael in Felicity's room. I had hoped, but it seemed too easy. It was more likely that he'd already skipped town, not caring about the sheriff's instruction to stay put. He hadn't stayed in the jail cell, so why should now be any different?

And yet, a man's voice called, "Is that you, Fiz?"

Cute nickname.

Now, how to make myself sound forty years younger.

I covered my mouth with the sleeve of my blouse to muffle my voice and said, "I forgot my key."

A pause.

And then the door opened.

No surprises. No twists to the story. It was almost disappointing, seeing Michael Richards standing in front of me, looking far more surprised to see me than I was to see him.

"I'm sorry, I think you have the wrong room," he said, obviously not recognizing me. And why would he? I was a random old woman he'd seen in passing on one occasion.

I gave him a smile as I bustled past him, Skittles nestled in my arms. "It's the right one. This is Felicity's room, correct?"

Michael turned and stared after me, the door still wide open. "It is, but she's not here right now."

"I can wait." And then I settled myself on the edge of the bed. Skittles leaped up and settled in next to me. "You don't by any chance have water I could give my cat, do you?"

Michael looked at Skittles, seemingly wanting to kick us out but not quite knowing how. "Of course," he finally said, shutting the door and then finding a paper bowl and filling it from the sink. He placed it on the floor next to the bed, and Skittles immediately jumped down and began lapping from it.

"I like your tattoos," I said, nodding to his arm. "Very distinctive. You must love Halloween."

"Halloween?" he asked, distracted by the mess Skittles was making with the water.

"Yes. Because of the skeleton."

His gaze moved from Skittles to me, then to his tattoo. "It's more of a statement," he said.

"I see. And what statement are you trying to make?"

He cocked his head to the side. "Who are you again?"

"Jo Darby," I said, sticking out a hand. "Felicity and I met on the day of the competition, and she's been absolutely lovely. I'm hoping she can stop by my bakery so I can give her some pastries before you all leave tomorrow."

Michael took my hand and shook it, not seeming to know how he'd gotten himself into this situation. "Nice to meet you, Jo, and I'm more than happy to pass on the message to Felicity."

"I appreciate that," I said. "But I'll wait. Call me old school, but I like face-to-face interactions. For example, without stopping by in person, I wouldn't have realized what kind eyes you have. They tell me that you're someone I can trust. Not at all what I was expecting with all the gossip that's being spread out there."

His gaze immediately jumped to the door, as if he were expecting the police to burst in. "What have you heard?"

I preferred that he not know I was aware he was running from the law—he didn't seem dangerous, but I really didn't want to push my luck. I patted Skittles on top of her head, like I wasn't at all worried about the direction this conversation had taken. "I've heard that you're the rebel in the surfing world." I nodded to his tattoo. "Like you said, you're making a statement."

Michael nodded slowly. "For better or for worse."

"From the frown on your face, I'd say it's for worse. Are you sure it's a statement worth making?"

Michael stayed quiet for a moment, thinking. How easily so many of us chose rebellion, even when most didn't know what they were rebelling against.

Not me. I was very aware what I was rebelling against. I chose to dye my hair because I was rebelling against old age. I couldn't fight aging itself, and I had certainly been feeling it over the past few years, but that didn't mean I had to embrace it.

"Yes, it is worth it," Michael finally said. "You asked what kind of statement I'm trying to make." He glanced down at Skittles and saw the bowl was empty of water, but the carpet was thoroughly soaked. He retrieved a towel from the bathroom, then placed it under the bowl.

"When I announced to my family that I was going to pursue surfing professionally, they laughed at me," he said. "I had been sick as a child and was pale and skinny. My family told me I should focus on things I could be good at. An office job, maybe. Something that didn't take a lot of energy." He paused. "Looking back, I think my mom was more worried than anything. Even though I went out surfing every day like the rest of the kids in Florida, she thought I wasn't strong enough. That I would be injured."

"That must have been hard," I said, "not having anyone believe in you."

Michael gave a little nod, then sat down on the bed next to me. "When my older brother and I were kids, he liked to be mean just for the fun of it. Tormented me any chance he got. One day when we were at the swimming pool, he casually glanced over at me and he said, 'Mikey, I don't know why you even leave the house. You look like death itself. Everyone notices—just look at them watching you, wondering if you're going to keel over at any moment.'" Michael's breath hitched. "It stuck with me—I'll never forget how serious he was in that moment. He wasn't just being mean. He believed it."

"That's so sad," I said, hating how awful people could be. It was even worse when it was the people who were supposed to love and protect us. I pointed to his tattoo. "Hence the skeleton. That's you on the surfboard."

Michael shifted on the bed. "The media—they made from it what they wanted. I didn't brand myself; they did. But I was advised to run with it, so I became this rebellious womanizer who puts down his opponents on national TV and doesn't care if he wins or loses."

"And how has that been working out for you?"

"Coaches won't work with me; sponsors want nothing to do with me. They see me as unpredictable. Bad for surfing."

"And your relationships with the other surfers?" I asked.

Michael shrugged. "Depends on which ones you talk to. Golden boys like your local hero, Isaac, or Bryce Carlton—they're the same as everyone else. Won't give me a chance. Gotta protect their images."

I gave him a kind smile. "To be fair, you did spread the rumor that Bryce was cheating and paying off the judges."

Michael stood up and threw his arms in the air. "One comment—one stupid remark, and it will follow me around until the day I die. I was speaking off the cuff, doing my usual bit. A reporter asked what I thought of Bryce, and I said, 'His scores are good. Too good. I wouldn't be surprised if he's paying off the judges.'" Michael rubbed his eyebrows, like he was getting tired just thinking about it. "The media ran with it, and Bryce had that nightmare chasing him for the rest of his career."

"Did you ever consider apologizing?" I asked as Michael began pacing the room.

"I tried, but he wouldn't take my call." Michael turned to me. "Bryce was a good guy. He didn't deserve what I did to him. But as loud as I was—as much as I tried telling people that I had made it all up, no one would listen. They'd created their own narrative by then, and it was ever-evolving. I no longer had control of it. And I'll regret it forever."

I looked around the room. "Not enough regret to not date his girlfriend, though."

I didn't know why I'd said it. It was harsh, and a bit below the belt. I prided myself on being the nice one, and that remark was certainly against my nature.

But there was something about Michael I didn't understand. He told a good story, but his actions went far beyond a good branding strategy. No marketing team had made him so drunk that he'd run down Main Street waving a gun—no one else had gotten him arrested. He'd managed that quite nicely on his own.

"Felicity has nothing to do with this," Michael nearly yelled, struggling to keep his temper under control. He turned a fierce gaze on me. "Why are you really here? Because I know that Felicity wasn't expecting you, and she won't be back for hours."

I tried pushing myself up from the bed but was struggling to catch my balance. I held out a hand. "Help me, would you?"

Michael stared at me for a moment before ultimately stepping forward and taking my hand. He was gentle, a stark contrast to his outburst.

Once I was standing, I turned to face him. "Michael, I believe that, overall, you're a good man. And Felicity must see something special in you if she helped you escape from jail. But what on earth would possess you to storm the sheriff's station like that? You were under no suspicion until you did that. Now you're a fugitive, and they are looking at you for the murder of Bryce Carlton. Especially because you practically demanded that they consider you a suspect."

Michael's whole demeanor seemed to crumble. "Because people thought I hated the man. Reporters were shoving their cameras in my face, asking if it was a relief to know that he was finally out of the picture. That he couldn't cheat anymore. That he was no longer a threat to the sport of surfing." He pulled in a shaky breath. "They expected I'd agree with them. There was one woman in general—it almost seemed like she was trying to lead me into a trap. Almost like she wanted me to confess that this was what I'd wanted all along." He looked at me. "I needed people to know that I was demanding justice for Bryce. That I didn't wish him harm. After all the dumb stuff I've said in the past, I needed them to know."

"That may be, but there was no need to storm the sheriff's station. Isaac was locked up—as far as you knew, justice was being served."

Michael chuckled softly, but his eyes were sad. "Isaac didn't kill Bryce. I know they didn't get along. And yes, Isaac bought into all those cheating rumors. But Isaac is as decent as they come. I mean, you saw it—he's the one who pulled Bryce out of the water. Whatever their rivalry, Isaac didn't want Bryce dead."

I was quiet for a moment. I believed Michael.

"So, who did want him dead?" I asked, more to myself than to Michael.

Michael walked to the door and placed a hand on the doorknob, indicating our time together was over. "I don't have the faintest idea. And honestly, at this point, I don't care." When I raised a surprised eyebrow, he gave me an apologetic smile. "It's been a long few days, Mrs..."

"Jo," I prompted.

"Jo. And I just want to go home and try to put all this in the past. I know it won't be that easy. That it will plague the surfing community for years. The mystery behind his death will be a constant source of conversation. But...I'm tired, and I just want to continue doing what I love. Surfing. If that means I keep up the rebellious image, so be it. If that means people speculate that I'm the one who killed Bryce, fine. It's not like I get sponsorships anyway. But I just want to move on."

It seemed to me that Michael Richards should care a little bit more than he claimed to, but I could also tell that he was telling the truth. He was exhausted, his eyes red and the bags under his eyes dark. He'd spent many restless nights since Bryce's death.

"I understand that," I said. "It takes an emotional, and physical, toll—caring." I paused. "I'm sorry to press like this, but you can't think of a single person that had a disagreement with Bryce, or even ill feelings toward him?"

Michael raised a shoulder. "He received angry letters from fans from time to time, but we all receive those. If we so much as get a haircut they don't like, they take it personally. With how many competitions I've lost lately, you can imagine how many letters I've been getting."

"Your fans aren't happy with you?"

"Livid."

"But Bryce didn't lose," I said. "Ever."

"No, he didn't," Michael agreed. "Doesn't mean he didn't get letters, though." He motioned to the door.

"I'm sorry for your loss," I told him, moving away from the bed and giving Skittles' leash a soft tug. She stood and then stretched. It was accompanied by a giant yawn. "I wish you safe travels tomorrow, and I will be cheering from afar. You're going to do great things in your career, I'm sure of it."

He gave me a kind smile. "If only the rest of the country believed in me as much as you do." He opened the door. "Good luck, Jo. And for the record, I do hope you catch whoever killed Bryce. He deserves that much."

I moved to leave, but there in the open doorway stood Felicity, her room key in her hand, as if she was just about to use it.

Her lips parted in surprise as she took in my presence. Her gaze then moved to Michael, who stood just behind me. Her eyes narrowed slightly. "It looks like we've got a problem."

18

Michael didn't seem the least bit bothered by Felicity's presence. "Perfect timing. Jo was just looking for you, Fiz. I didn't think you'd be back for a few hours, at least."

"Forgot my water bottle," Felicity said, moving past me into the room. She turned. "But funny that you were looking for me, Jo, considering you'd left me in the dining room only a few minutes ago. I hadn't gone anywhere." She eyed Skittles, who was pulling on the leash, trying to leave the room. Now that I'd gotten her moving, she was ready for another adventure.

"Jo believes me," Michael said. "She doesn't think I killed Bryce, and she wants to help."

Felicity folded her arms across her chest. "Of course she doesn't think you killed him. It's me she suspects. Jo was trying to get information from you."

Michael's eyes widened for the briefest of moments before he released a cannon-like laugh. When neither Felicity nor I joined him, his gaze bounced between us. "Wait, you're serious?" He spun toward me. "Felicity would never kill Bryce. For all his faults, she loved him and gave everything to help him succeed." He paused. "Is that why you were really here—you wanted me to tell you that Felicity had murdered Bryce?"

The hurt in his eyes, it was unbearable.

"No." I said it too quickly, and it made me seem guilty. "The truth is that I thought if I found you, it would lead me closer to discovering who had killed Bryce. That's all I'm looking for—clues. I thought it was possible that the same person who had broken you out of jail was our murderer. But that's all it was. A possibility."

Felicity shook her head. "Why would you take something like that upon yourself? A woman of your age should be enjoying retirement, or at the very least focusing on managing your bakery. Not running around town looking for a murderer, throwing accusations on every stranger she meets." She paused. "Please don't tell the sheriff that Michael is here. He didn't do anything wrong. And they'll arrest him. Lock him up. He doesn't deserve that."

I gave her a sad smile. "He was drunk, threatened the sheriff with a gun, acted like a lunatic, and for what? To make a statement." I glanced at Michael. "You're lucky you weren't shot."

Michael shrugged. "You're not wrong."

"That being said," I continued, "I'm not going to tell the sheriff. That would only complicate things—muddy the waters, if you will."

Felicity's features relaxed, and she released a long breath. "Thank goodness for that."

"But I do have to ask," I continued, "is it true that you and Michael were dating behind Bryce's back?" Before they could protest, I held up my hands in a defensive gesture. "I don't judge, mind you. It's just that it does make Michael look quite guilty."

"Michael and I—we started as friends," Felicity said. "Have been for years. Bryce and I had a bit of a falling out a few months back. We broke up. But Lindi thought it best that we act like we were still together. At least until competition season ends. And yes, during that time, Michael and I grew to be more than friends. We started dating, and we figured some public flirting couldn't hurt, because Michael flirts with everyone. A couple years back, he actually had his sights set on one of the female surfers, but she wouldn't give him the time of day. To avoid embarrassment, he pretended that he couldn't care less and started hitting on every good-looking woman he saw. It helped his brand, I'll tell you that."

"Hey," Michael protested. "That's my personal business."

Felicity threw him an amused glance. "Serves you right. Who knows what you told Jo before I arrived. Besides, it led to a happy ending. You realized that you hated all that surface-level stuff and that it had been me you'd wanted all along." She glanced at me, and her smile dipped. "In all seriousness, whatever Michael told you before I arrived, you should probably just forget about it. Like Michael said, it's our personal business."

"Even the angry fan mail?" I asked.

Felicity's gaze snapped to Michael. "You told her about that? If Bryce were alive, he'd—"

"But he's not, is he?" Michael interrupted. He turned back to me. "We've all had it drilled into us to not make a big deal about those letters. That they don't mean anything, and that bringing attention to them makes the problem worse. We don't answer them, and we don't talk about them to the media." He glanced at Felicity. "But what if—"

Felicity spoke over him. "Bryce wasn't worried about it."

"It was hand-delivered," Michael said, his voice dropping just above a whisper. "That makes this one different."

Felicity took an angry step toward Michael. "And let's say we tell the sheriff about the letter. What if he tracks the angry fan down and it's a twelve-year-old girl in Oklahoma and now she's in trouble with the police—*we* got her in trouble. Soon the news is saying we're harassing a little girl. What then?"

Michael was quiet for a minute. "You really think it had nothing to do with Bryce's death?"

Felicity gave an aggressive nod. "I'm sure of it."

I wanted to raise my hand and work my way into the conversation, but keeping Skittles from charging out of the room had become quite a chore, and, now that I thought about it, I was getting tired. I moved to a high-back chair in the corner and lowered myself into it. Skittles made another escape attempt before giving up and ultimately curling up at my feet.

"Not to be a bother," I said. Felicity's and Michael's heads both swiveled toward me, as if they'd forgotten I was there. "What exactly was this person angry about?"

Neither spoke right away.

"Well?" I pressed. "What was it? If it's something that can help get Michael and Isaac out of this predicament—because don't think that just leaving town will allow you to move on, Michael. You're a fugitive now—but if it's something that can help, you really should tell me."

Felicity hesitated.

"It had to do with those love triangle rumors you've heard," Michael finally said. "This particular fan thought that Felicity was cheating on Bryce with me. They threatened that if Bryce didn't dump Felicity—because he deserved better—they would have to step in and take matters into their own hands."

"It really was insane," Felicity said, the fight seeming to have left her. "Bryce was used to threatening letters, but this was the first time someone had threatened me."

This had just gotten more concerning. Twelve-year-old girl or not, we needed to go to the sheriff with this.

"What did Bryce have to say about the letter?" I asked, thinking back to the day of the competition and Bryce's apparent lack of interest in his girlfriend.

Felicity and Michael shared a long look.

"Come now, you might as well tell me everything," I said, getting impatient with all these secrets.

Felicity glanced at me. "I didn't see who delivered the letter—Bryce had received quite a few letters the evening before the competition. I only knew of it because my sister had been going through all of them, putting them in a manilla envelope for Bryce to read later, after the competition. Even the letters he personally takes from fans, he doesn't read them until the flight back home. You know what he was like—always had to stay in the zone. Anyway, when Lindi discovered the threatening letter, she immediately showed it to me—told me to be careful."

My mind whirled, and I sat up straight, accidentally kicking Skittles as I did so. I'd forgotten she was there. She yawned, then rolled over so she was belly up, and then went back to sleep. "You're telling me that Bryce never even knew about it?"

Felicity shook her head. "I didn't want him to worry."

"And why didn't you take them to the sheriff the moment something happened to Bryce? Weren't you worried for your own safety? It doesn't matter if it was a twelve-year-old girl, not if you're being threatened."

Felicity had the decency to look embarrassed, and she mumbled something.

I shook my head. "You're going to have to speak louder than that. I'm an old woman, and I can't hear a thing."

"Because there was no point," Felicity said louder. "As soon as the sheriff read that letter, the press would catch wind of it. There would be a huge scandal, and my name would be splashed across the news with lies, because you know they would take that letter out of context."

I stared. "You're telling me that you were in danger and you didn't go to the authorities because you were worried about what people would say about you?"

Felicity's gaze dropped. "It sounds dumb when you say it like that."

"That's because it is." I knew my words were harsh, and I hated seeing the effect they had on Felicity—tears pooling in her eyes—but that letter would have changed the entire course of the sheriff's investigation. Isaac never would have been arrested, Michael would never have felt the need to storm the sheriff's office, and the real murderer might have already been behind bars by now.

I moved to stand but found myself stuck in the chair. My legs had given out on me again. It was climbing those stairs that had done it, I was sure. No more exercise for me for at least the next week. It was bad for my health. With a little help from Michael, I managed to get back on my feet.

"Can I see the letters Bryce received that night?" I asked. "All of them."

19

My heart beat fast as I impatiently waited for Felicity to dig the letters out of the bottom of her suitcase, where she'd hidden them. "Only touch the edges," I said, though I doubted it mattered anymore. The murderer had likely wiped the letter clean, and Lindi's and Felicity's fingerprints would already be covering it.

Felicity soon returned with a manilla folder. She hesitated before handing it over to me. "I was hoping to keep Bryce's memory intact. If this letter gets out, his death will be associated with—"

"Justice," I finished for her. "Unless you'd rather we didn't find his killer." I met her gaze, refusing to look away.

Her gaze dropped, and she handed me the envelope. "You're right, of course."

I pulled the stack of papers from the folder and spread them out on the bed. There were about fifteen of them. At first glance, all of the letters seemed different. Different handwriting, different paper, even different perfumes had been sprayed on them. The combined smell of all of them made me lightheaded, and I had to sit down.

I started reading them—most were generic wishes of good luck. One of them, signed by a woman named M.H., gushed over how brave he was out on the waves, never letting fear rule him—only his passion. It went into some other details that made me blush, so I pushed it aside.

Then there was the woman who had had the audacity to cover hers in glitter. It had already transferred to my hands and to the bedspread before I realized it. "If you ask me, this one is the killer," I said. "Candace Palmer."

"But that's the nicest letter of them all," Felicity said. "She even wrote a poem about Bryce and everything."

I scrunched my nose as I wiped my hands on the bedspread. It only made it worse. "Glitter is the tool of a psycho."

Felicity's lips quirked up at the corners, but then they dropped again. She pointed to a letter that was partially hidden by the glitter bomb letter. "That's the one threatening him."

I pulled it out but didn't read it—not even a quick skim.

Because there on the bottom of the letter was a name I recognized.

Juliette Bigsby. The star-struck reporter.

My body might not have been as strong as it used to be,

but I'd thought my mind was still able to keep up well enough. Right now, though, it was spinning. The clues didn't add up. Sure, she was one of Bryce's biggest fans, but would she actually murder him because she thought he deserved a better girlfriend?

I ran through all of our interactions together—anything that would provide a hint that she was capable of this.

There were none.

But this letter—it was what had been missing from the investigation. It was what we needed to put away Bryce's murderer.

"If you'll excuse me," I said, "I have someplace to be. Would you mind calling the sheriff on your cellular phone? Tell him to come to the bed and breakfast, and that it's urgent."

"You know who did it—who killed Bryce, don't you?" Michael said.

I was saved from answering when Isaac burst into the room.

"Don't you dare lay a finger on—" Isaac's words left him when he saw Michael. His gaze then moved to Felicity, then me, and then Skittles, who shot across the floor and under the bed. I hadn't even realized I was no longer holding her leash.

I smiled at Isaac's heroic attempt at saving me.

"I'm all right, Isaac. But we really should get going if we're going to wrap up this murder before anyone leaves town." I glanced past him into the hallway. "Where's Dottie?"

"Using my phone to call Sheriff Hart." Isaac didn't move to leave, instead crossing his arms over his chest, daring anyone to try to get past him. "On the security footage, we saw Felicity take handfuls of the candy, which was enough to suspect she was Bryce's murderer. But then we saw her sneaking Michael up the stairs. He was in disguise, but he didn't bother covering up his tattoo. We tried to find you so we could tell you what we'd discovered, but when Mrs. Warner told us you'd come up to Felicity's room—"

"You feared the worst," I finished for him. "Thank you for calling the sheriff, because we'll certainly be needing him, but Felicity didn't kill Bryce."

Isaac's gaze took in Felicity and Michael, his forehead scrunching up, like he didn't believe me.

"I know what we saw," he finally said.

"And if I had been with you two, watching the same security footage you had, I would have come to the same conclusion," I assured him as I walked over to the bed, reached down, and grabbed hold of Skittles' leash. It was just barely sticking out from under the bed, and I gave it a gentle tug, prompting the cat to come back out—though not without some protesting. "However," I continued, "based on new evidence, I think you are wrong."

Isaac still didn't move. "But you're not sure."

I approached Isaac, Skittles grudgingly following me.

"There are a few missing pieces, but I think I have the general gist of what happened." I glanced at Felicity and Michael. "When I said we have somewhere we need to be, I was referring to you two as well. You'll want to be present for what happens next."

Isaac threw them a suspicious glance, but then stepped aside. "You know that if you try anything, Michael, I'm stronger. You won't win."

Michael gave him a lopsided grin. "I wouldn't dare try."

Isaac picked up Skittles as we paraded past him. "We'll be faster if I carry her."

I patted him on the arm. "I've always said you're one of the good ones."

"Where are we going?" Felicity asked as we descended the spiral staircase.

I hadn't quite gotten that far. I didn't really want to do this publicly and hoped the dining room had cleared out from breakfast. When we neared the bottom, Lindi Fierce came into view. She was waiting in the entryway for her sister, checking her phone and tapping her foot impatiently. When she saw the four of us on the staircase, she froze, her lips parting in surprise.

She glanced around the entryway, making sure we were alone. "What is he doing out here?" she said in a fierce whisper. "We said he'd lie low until we left tomorrow."

"He's not in danger of being arrested," I said, my voice strong and confident. I suddenly wondered if that was true. He hadn't killed Bryce, but he had threatened the sheriff with a gun. That might still warrant some jail time. I didn't like the thought of that nice young man being locked up, though. Maybe I could sway the sheriff to go easy on him.

Lindi studied me, her eyes suspicious. "And why is that?"

"Because the sheriff has bigger things to worry about," I said.

We had just reached the bottom of the staircase when the door to the bed and breakfast flew open. Sheriff Hart and Deputy Randy rushed in and slammed the door on an onslaught of reporters who had followed them there. A man with a camera managed to stick his foot in the doorway, preventing the door from shutting. A yowl of pain came from the other side of the door.

"They caught wind that something might be going down," Sheriff Hart said, his breaths coming fast.

I walked to the partially open door, the cameraman's foot still wedged in the crack. "Is Juliette Bigsby out there with you?" I asked the cameraman.

"I'm here," she called from the back of the pack.

I made eye contact with the cameraman. "You're going to let her through, and she will be the only one allowed inside." He protested, of course, likely fearing for his job if he gave in too easily. "I could always have you arrested," I said with a smile.

Another dirty look and he removed his foot, allowing

Juliette to pass by. When her cameraman tried to follow suit, I slammed the door shut and locked it.

Juliette now looked like she'd be the one protesting, but I held up a finger. "I said you were the only one allowed."

Sheriff Hart was looking less winded but more annoyed. "What is all of this, Jo? Dottie wouldn't say over the phone. Just told me I needed to get here as quickly as possible."

"We have proof that Felicity is your murderer," Dottie said, walking into the room. She looked exhausted and was limping, but her eyes held fire. "She was hiding Michael Richards in her room upstairs."

Sheriff Hart scanned the entryway, and his gaze landed on Michael, who was trying to make himself small as he hid behind Issac. For a moment I was sure Michael was going to run, but then his gaze landed on the front door, and I was sure he was thinking of all those reporters out there. He thought better of it and instead sat down on the bottom step of the staircase, seemingly resigned to his fate.

"Nice work," the sheriff said, "though I have to say I'm a bit confused. You had told Deputy Randy that Michael was in Lindi Fierce's room. Busted in like I owned the place, only to come away with nothing."

I gave him a sheepish smile. "Yes, I'm sorry about that. It's taken a while to work everything out."

Sheriff Hart took out his handcuffs and stepped toward Felicity. "Murdering your boyfriend and then harboring a fugitive. You've been busy. I'll take your full statement back at the station."

Felicity threw a panicked look in my direction, and I hurried forward. "You have it wrong, sheriff. Felicity didn't kill Bryce, and neither did Michael. The most I think you could arrest him for is drunk and disorderly conduct."

Sheriff Hart released a disbelieving laugh. "He threatened us with a gun."

I nodded. "Yes, that was the disorderly part."

Juliette took a step toward the door, as though just now realizing that she was not here as a reporter but as a suspect. "You know, I really should get back to my hotel. Lots to do before I leave tomorrow. I'll let someone else get the story this time."

Sheriff Hart held up a hand. "You're staying put until I find out what's actually happening here." He glanced at Deputy Randy. "Stand in front of the door, please. If anyone tries leaving, stop them by any means necessary."

"That seems a little dramatic," Dottie said, then glanced at me. "Didn't Isaac tell you what was on those videos?"

"Yes, but you didn't have all of the information. You didn't know that Felicity and Lindi are sisters—different last names, you see. That's the first big clue. Anyone can change their name willy nilly, and you'd never know." I paused, realizing I'd made a big mistake. Things weren't at all how I'd thought.

"And the second?" Dottie prompted me.

Right. "The second clue is that you didn't have the letters."

Every head snapped toward me, but only two faces went pale.

Juliette's bottom lip began to tremble. "Do you mean my letters? We only wanted to wish Bryce good luck."

I gave her a kind smile. "I know you did, and you'll be able to keep that memory forever, just like you said."

"You're saying that the reporter killed Bryce?" Sheriff Hart asked, looking incredulous.

Every eye was on me as I said, "No. She's completely innocent." I turned to the only other pale face in the room. "I'm saying that someone wanted it to look like she did."

"Enough of the riddles, Jo," Sheriff Hart said, getting impatient. "You called me here, so either tell me why, or I'm leaving. I don't have time to run in circles, guessing what you've discovered. If you hadn't noticed, I have a murder to solve by tomorrow morning."

I supposed that was fair.

"I don't know why she did it," I said. "But Lindi Fierce killed Bryce Carlton."

Of course, Lindi immediately denied it. So adamantly that I wondered if I'd made a mistake.

Was it possible that I was wrong?

20

F elicity's face slackened, and she turned to her sister. "You wouldn't do something so terrible, right? Tell me you didn't do it."

Lindi merely rolled her eyes. "Oh, stop. Of course I didn't kill Bryce. Like the old lady said, I have no motive, not when Bryce helped my career as much as he did. That guy made me a lot of money."

I glanced between the two sisters, now unsure of the premise behind my entire accusation. I decided to move forward with it and see where it led. The worst that could happen was that I was wrong.

At least, I hoped that was the worst that could happen.

"Juliette Bigsby," I said, clasping my hands behind my back and walking across the large entryway, "a reporter, who happens to be Bryce's number one fan, hand-delivered a pile of letters the night before the competition." I stopped in front of Lindi. "You'd already decided to kill Bryce at that point, but you needed someone to take the fall—someone who would take suspicion off you, because, naturally, you would be the sheriff's primary suspect. As Bryce's coach, you probably spent even more time with him than your sister did. It needed to be someone else."

Lindi laughed, like I'd told a joke. "Is that right?"

I nodded, certain of it. "Yes, it is. You were there when Juliette gave him the letters and you saw the manatee tattoo on the inside of her wrist. She'd be perfect. Bryce never read his fan letters until after the competition, so you looked through his letters for one with Juliette's name on it. You planned to destroy it and then replace it with the one you'd written. The one that would make her appear to be Bryce's killer. Only you didn't find a letter with Juliette's name on it—I don't know why you didn't question that—she was his biggest fan, after all. But you ignored that little voice that said something didn't add up and simply added your own fabricated letter to the pile."

"Can you believe this lady?" Lindi asked Felicity with another laugh. She turned back to me. "Maybe it's time for the retirement home."

"Hey," Dottie shouted, taking a threatening step toward Lindi. "No one threatens my sister with a retirement home except for me."

Sheriff Hart placed himself between the two women.

"Go on, Jo. But you might want to get to the point a little faster."

"Of course." I turned my attention back to Lindi. "What you didn't know is that Juliette had indeed written a letter, but she couldn't have anyone connecting her to Bryce's fan club. People wouldn't take her seriously, professionally speaking. She decided to use her initials instead—her real ones. M.H., for Margaret Hayes. I'll admit that it took far too long for me to piece things together on that. It was very clever."

Felicity's eyes widened slightly, and they filled with moisture. "Oh my gosh, you did do it, didn't you. I knew you'd been acting weird these past few days, but I just thought it was because of Bryce's death—that you were torn up about it."

Lindi's eyes narrowed, and she made a lunge for me. At the same time that the sheriff caught her midair, Skittles appeared out of nowhere and leaped onto Lindi's back.

"Get it off," she screeched, writhing and attempting to loosen the cat's grip. Skittles' claws held tight until Sheriff Hart managed to tear Skittles off, ripping Lindi's shirt in the process.

"I'm so sorry," Isaac said, rushing forward at the same time Dottie said:

"Good job, Skittles! There's that protective instinct kicking in. She knows the bad from the good."

Isaac took Skittles from the Sheriff's arms. "She leapt out of my arms before I realized what was happening."

"And I'll pretend to be angry about it," the sheriff said, placing a firm hand on Lindi's shoulder. "Now, back to the matter at hand."

Lindi twisted, trying to see the damage done to her back. "I'm sure my wounds are infected." She looked at me. "I'll sue you over it, and I'll make sure that demon cat of yours is put down."

I folded my arms across my chest. "I'd like to see you try."

"Like I said, we're moving on." Sheriff Hart looked at me.

"Right." I narrowed my eyes at Lindi. "You kept the letters hidden in the bottom of your suitcase, though I'm not sure why if your plan was to frame Miss Bigsby."

Lindi no longer denied her involvement, instead staring me down, her gaze intense. Her whole body radiated fury—like she was a nuclear reactor that was about to blow. "Backup plan," she said, not seeming at all sorry. "With Isaac and Michael under suspicion, it didn't make sense to put myself in the spotlight by presenting new evidence."

Juliette had been quietly taking everything in from the side of the room, where she had pressed herself up against the wall, almost like she was trying to become invisible. When I glanced her way, I could see the trails of tears running down her cheeks.

"Why?" she asked, her voice cracking. "I don't even know you."

"No, but I know you," Lindi said, her voice dripping with disgust. "You've been hanging around here since two days before the competition started and you, a grown woman, were throwing yourself at Bryce like a lovesick teenager. You even had a tattoo matching the manatee on his surfboard. When I saw that pile of letters you delivered the night before the competition, I knew you'd be perfect."

I turned back to Lindi, grief for Juliette welling in my chest. It wasn't fair that she had been caught up in this. She'd told me the greatest night of her life had been hand-delivering those letters, and it had led to this nightmare.

"That doesn't answer the question of why you had to kill him at all," I said, my voice quiet. "Is it because Bryce really had been cheating in his competitions?"

"It wasn't him who was cheating," a low voice said from the direction of the dining room. Judge Pence stepped from around the corner. "Bryce had no idea what Lindi was doing, the poor guy. I was assigned to all of Bryce's competitions after accusations started swirling that he was paying off the judges. It was my job to look for corruption."

"And you found it," Sheriff Hart said.

Michael shook his head. "He couldn't have. I made it up—there was no truth to it."

Judge Pence threw a glance his way. "You might have been speaking off the cuff, but that doesn't make my findings any less true. It was very subtle, and it took me a long time to understand how she was doing it." He paused and looked at Lindi. "Shall I tell them, or would you like to?"

She waved a hand through the air, like it didn't matter anymore.

"Very well." The judge turned back to the sheriff. "It was as simple as the power of suggestion. Most evenings during competitions, athletes and coaches head to local restaurants or bars to relax and unwind from their busy day. Lindi paid random locals who were already fans of Bryce to go into these bars when they knew the judges would be there and talk amongst themselves about how incredible Bryce's form was and how he tackled the waves more smoothly than any other surfer in the competition."

Judge Pence raised a shoulder. "You get enough of these people talking about how amazing Bryce is, every evening, and even though you are an expert in your field, it starts to color your worldview. It doesn't flip it upside down, mind you. If a judge couldn't stand Bryce before, it wouldn't make them his biggest fan. But even if those positive comments only increased Bryce's scores by half a point, it was just enough to give him the edge."

"Using psychology to help your surfer win. That's brilliant," I said. "And nearly undetectable." Every head turned to look at me, and I felt heat rush up my neck. "Terrible, of course. No doubt about that. But still, you have to admire the brilliance behind it."

"Let me guess," Sheriff Hart said, turning back to the judge. "Bryce found out, and he wasn't happy about it."

Judge Pence shook his head. "That's the sad part. As far as I can tell, he never even suspected—Lindi only thought he knew. And if Bryce fired his coach and told people what was really going on, both his and Lindi's careers would be ruined; they'd never recover from something like that."

"So she decided to get rid of him before that could happen," Sheriff Hart said. He glanced at Lindi. "And you dragged your sister into it, convincing her to feed him oatmeal with poisonous berries." He approached her, shaking his head like a disappointed parent. "Turn around and place your hands behind your back."

I always got the feeling that the sheriff hated this part.

Michael shot to his feet and was at Felicity's side before Deputy Randy managed to get the handcuffs on her too. "Felicity had nothing to do with this."

"It's true. I had no idea," Felicity said, her expression panicked. "I knew Lindi wanted to be known as the best coach in the world. She liked the fame and the money. The respect. But I didn't know she would go this far."

Lindi snorted as the sheriff led her toward the door. "You only pretended to not see what was happening—how Bryce was really winning. You were in the same bars and listening to the same conversations I was."

Felicity was now in tears, clinging onto Michael, like he could protect her. "I swear I didn't. If I had, I would have put a stop to it. Bryce and I might have fallen out of love, but that didn't mean I didn't care about him."

At her sister's words, Lindi stopped, refusing to take another step. She turned toward her sister. "You're telling the truth? You really didn't know about the cheating?"

Felicity gave a vigorous shake of her head.

Lindi released a long breath, then straightened and looked the sheriff in the eyes. "Release my sister. It was me who killed Bryce Carlton, and me only. I will plead guilty, whatever it takes."

"Why?" the sheriff asked, sounding skeptical. In truth, so was I. That was a quick turnaround.

Lindi didn't answer right away, though she looked like she wanted to say more.

"What?" I prompted.

Her gaze met mine. "I deserve to be in prison, and my sister doesn't. It's as simple as that. Because—" She pulled in another long breath. "I placed the belladonna berries in Felicity's oatmeal too, just in case Bryce ate the wrong bowl. It just so happened that you came along with your bread pudding, and she left with you instead of eating her breakfast. You saved Felicity's life."

Felicity stared. "You were okay with me dying to ensure that Bryce did?"

For the first time, Lindi really did look sorry for what she'd done. "I thought you knew what I'd been doing," she whispered. "And you just admitted that if you'd known, you would have had no qualms turning me in. You were always the one with the conscience when we were growing up, always telling Mom and Dad on me, and I couldn't risk it. Not now. It would have ruined me. Everything I've built."

Felicity was stunned into silence, merely watching as

Sheriff Hart led Lindi out of the building. Deputy Randall stepped away from Felicity and replaced the handcuffs in his belt. She immediately fell to her knees, sobbing.

Deputy Randall squatted next to her and lightly touched her shoulder. "We'll need you to come down to the station when you're feeling up to it. Need to get your official statement. But not right now. Take whatever time you need."

He didn't wait for a response before nodding to me in farewell, and then he followed the sheriff.

"I should head up to my room," Judge Pence said, taking a step back. "This is a PR nightmare for the surfing community, and I have some calls to make. We'll heal from it, though. Eventually."

I was sure it would take even longer than he anticipated. When I turned back to Felicity, I saw that Michael had lowered himself onto the floor and was cradling her in his arms. He buried his head in her hair, telling her everything was going to be okay.

What I would have given for someone like that when I had been younger—someone who would always have my back, no matter what.

Maybe I shouldn't have dismissed romance so easily— dismissed the opportunity to have a partner in life, someone who would stay by my side through thick and thin.

Of course, even as I thought it, I knew that kind of love

was rare, and not for me. I was grateful that Felicity had found it.

Michael stood, still holding Felicity's hand as he helped her off the floor. He looked at me. "Thank you, Jo, for believing in us."

I gave him an embarrassed smile. "I don't know that I did much."

"Neither Felicity nor I are in jail right now, so I'd say that's plenty."

That was true, but it felt wrong to take all the credit. I couldn't have done it without everyone else's help. They were the ones who had provided the information and the context; I had just put it all together in a neat little package. And it hadn't even been all that neat. It had been quite messy, actually.

"What's next for you two?" I asked.

Felicity looked at Michael, tears still flowing from her questioning eyes.

Michael raised a shoulder. "I think it's time I rebranded myself—a new image. A real one. Felicity deserves that much. I can't go around pretending to be the womanizing rebel anymore. Not when I want to be so much more. Besides, there's always the chance that the sheriff will remember he was supposed to arrest me for drunk and disorderly conduct."

"I hope you learned your lesson," I said. "Nothing good comes from alcohol."

He laughed and pulled Felicity in, wrapping his arms

around her. Their gazes met, and it was like a scene from a movie. The kind that made you believe that forever love was real. "For the right motivation, I could be convinced."

He and Felicity pulled apart, he gave me a small wave and another thank you, and then they left the bed and breakfast—no more hiding. When they opened the front door, I noticed that the reporters were gone, apparently having chased after the sheriff when he'd left with Lindi. Everyone else who was still inside the bed and breakfast— we were old news.

Speaking of old news—I turned, looking for Isaac.

He was sitting next to Dottie on the staircase, Skittles curled up on his lap.

"Looks like you didn't need us," Dottie said to me. I couldn't tell how she meant it from the tone of her voice. It seemed almost wistful. "You would have made a wonderful detective back in the day."

"Of course I needed you," I said. "Without you—"

"You still would have found out about Lindi and Felicity being sisters and about the letter," Dottie finished for me. "You would have pieced it all together. You didn't need us."

I wasn't sure what to say to that. Dottie always said she didn't want to be a part of investigations. But now it seemed like she was feeling left out.

"I'm sorry that I didn't include you more," I said. "I should have waited for you instead of going up to Felicity's room by myself and—"

Isaac laughed and shook his head. "You did exactly as you needed to. And we're all better off for it. I'm sure Juliette is grateful as well."

Juliette. In all the commotion, I'd forgotten about her. I turned, searching her out, but the room was empty.

"She left shortly after the sheriff did," Dottie said. "I don't blame her, with everything that happened."

I nodded. "Yeah. Me neither."

"I do need your help with one more thing," Isaac said, squirming on the step he was seated on.

Dottie and I shared looks that said we both knew exactly what he needed help with, and we burst into laughter.

"Let me guess," Dottie said. "You need to use the bathroom, but you have a cat sleeping on your lap, and you'd feel guilty if you woke her."

Isaac grinned. "Pretty much."

"Welcome to our life," I said, then picked up the end of Skittles' leash and tugged. "Come on, girl. Naptime is over." For her, maybe. As for me, as soon as we returned home, I was crawling into bed. The day had barely started, and I was already exhausted.

Dottie glanced at her watch. "We should have opened the bakery by now, which means Autumn is probably trying to run the place by herself. We better hurry back."

I released a disappointed sigh and trudged toward the door. "What possessed us to start a bakery again?"

"Our sister's murder," Dottie replied.

Right. To the bakery, then. At least I knew there would be a fresh piece of bread pudding for me.

A thought struck me.

If our bread pudding had saved someone's life, which by all accounts it had, could we advertise it as such?

Life-saving pudding—yours could be next.

It had a nice ring to it.

21

B anging. Drilling. More banging. It filled the bakery.

"I can't work in these conditions," I said to Dottie, covering my ears with my hands. It didn't do anything. It was the shrill squeal of the drill that got me the most. Made me feel like I was at the dentist. My teeth hurt just listening to it.

A loud thud came from the direction of the staircase, and Dottie grimaced. "Let's just hope that everything is intact by the time Patty is finished."

The front door opened. Good thing we were already downstairs and sitting at the counter, because we couldn't hear the small bell above the door.

Juliette Bigsby.

"Patty, can you stop for a minute?" I yelled. "We have a customer."

The drilling continued.

"She'll never hear you," Dottie said, easing herself off her stool. "I'll tell her."

I held up a finger and smiled so that Juliette would know we were working on it. After another minute, the drilling stopped.

"Sounds like a construction zone in here," Juliette said with a laugh. She looked lighter than I'd seen her in days—practically glowing. And she'd dyed her hair.

"You look amazing," I told her. "And I love the blue streaks."

Juliette seemed self-conscious as she wound a lock of hair around a finger. "Felicity convinced me to do it, and I'm sure my boss is going to kill me, but if the last few days have taught me anything, it's that life is to be honored. Which is what brought me here."

"Honoring life brought you to our bakery? I'll take that as the highest compliment."

Dottie walked in from the back. "Patty's taking a thirty-minute break. Finally." She looked at Juliette and smiled. "Lovely to see you again. Sorry you had to come at a time like this. Patty, our doctor, is afraid that Jo and I are going to fall to our deaths while climbing the steps up to our apartment, and when she found out that our handyman is booked for the rest of the week, well, she took matters into her own hands. By this afternoon we should have a new handrail to cling onto."

"She sounds lovely," Juliette said.

"Yes, she is," I agreed. "Except, we're not entirely sure

how handy Patty is. We've heard quite a bit more yelling than we're used to, and it's taken her longer than we expected, as well. We're afraid to check on her progress, though. She keeps telling us to trust her."

"I love that," Juliette said, laughing. "Look, I won't keep you. It's just that I leave in a couple of hours, and I didn't thank you properly for everything you've done for me. Yesterday—it was too much, and I just ran. Didn't think. I just had to get out of there." Her gaze dropped. "I'm so embarrassed by the way I—"

Dottie held up a hand. "We'll have none of that. It was a traumatic experience, and you have nothing to apologize for."

Juliette's gaze lifted. "All the same. Thank you. I know I didn't always treat you right during our time together, and I'm not entirely convinced I've deserved how kind you've been to me."

"Nonsense. It's been our pleasure," I said. "But let's move on to the fun part of your visit."

Juliette blinked in confusion. "Fun part?"

"Yes. The part where I give you the éclairs that I promised you, and Dottie and I steal a couple for ourselves so we can all enjoy them together."

"Oh no, I couldn't," Juliette began, but Dottie's eyes had already lit up.

"That's the best idea you've had all day." And then she disappeared into the back.

"You can't say no now," I said with a laugh.

"No, I suppose not."

As Dottie returned, a tray of éclairs in hand, the front door swung open again, Jessie sprinting inside.

"What on earth is going on?" Dottie asked, nearly dropping the tray. She made it to the counter just in time. "Please tell me there hasn't been another murder."

"No, of course not," Jessie said, pulling in deep breaths. "You'll never believe who's back in town."

At this point, Dottie and I would believe just about anything, especially because we didn't know anyone who had left town. We hadn't lived here long enough.

"Who?" I asked, hoping she didn't actually expect us to guess.

"Leanne Warner."

Dottie and I gave her blank looks, which made Jessie look like she wanted to strangle us for not knowing what big news this was.

"Isaac's ex-fiancée," Jessie prompted. "Her parents own the bed and breakfast? She left for Hollywood and intended to only be gone for the summer, but she's been gone for two years? Any of that ringing a bell?"

Yikes. Yeah, we had heard of her, and how her leaving had nearly destroyed Isaac. I wondered how he was handling it. His ex-fiancée returning so soon after nearly being convicted of murder was terrible timing.

"Poor Leanne," Juliette said. "I doubt leaving Hollywood was her choice—that has to be so difficult."

Jessie turned to her, a hand on her hips. "I don't know

who you are, so I'll forgive you for that. Leanne should thank her lucky stars that she has a place like Starlight Ridge to come home to, and that Isaac is still here, and single no less. At this point, I'm tempted to say he deserves better, but everyone makes mistakes. We'll move past it, and they'll still get their fairytale ending. That's all that matters."

"Does Isaac agree?" Dottie asked. "I mean, she did leave him. Is he interested in rekindling what they had?"

Jessie looked between the three of us. "I can't believe it. You were the first ones I told, and it was wasted. I need to find someone who will appreciate the biggest news Starlight Ridge has ever had."

"A famous surfer was just murdered in our town, by his coach," I said. "That's pretty big news. You have seen all the reporters and news vans, right?"

Jessie waved a hand through the air. "That was a few days ago. And Leanne coming back to town—you'd understand if you grew up here. It means we're about to have the wedding of the century. I can't wait to make their cake."

And then she hurried out the door to find someone who loved gossip as much as she did. This was one of those times that I was reminded we hadn't grown up here, and we didn't always belong. Dottie and I were supposed to understand—we were supposed to be excited. But because we didn't have decades of backstory, we were left on the outside looking in.

Juliette reached for an éclair, her gaze on the front

window, where Jessie had stopped to talk to someone. "When I said I felt sorry for Leanne, it wasn't for the reasons that woman thought."

I grabbed an éclair for myself. "What do you mean?"

"As a reporter, I've heard the name Leanne Warner," Juliette said. "She's been working under a big screenwriter —been his pet project. She's made the gossip magazines a couple of times because she's been seen with some of the biggest names in Hollywood, and the rumblings are that a couple of them are interested in producing her screenplay. Her film is set in a town very similar to Starlight Ridge, so it's possible it could have been filmed right here, in your town."

I perked up at that. It had been a dream of mine to someday meet a famous actor.

"Ooh, that sounds exciting. So, why exactly are we feeling bad for Leanne, and why do you say it could have been filmed here—past tense?"

Juliette used her finger to wipe stray cream from her éclair and then licked it off. "Because if Leanne is back, that means things went south. The screenwriter she's been working under—he's known for throwing young hopefuls out the door when he gets bored of them. Rumor has it that he's looking for a screenwriter who can fill his shoes— shoes that he's deemed impossible to fill. Doesn't stop young screenwriters from trying, though."

Ouch. That did sound bad.

"As long as he keeps his drama in Hollywood," I said.

"That's the last thing we need—an arrogant celebrity throwing off our groove." I took a bite of my éclair. "Knowing our luck, next thing you know, we'll have another murder."

The End

CHOOSE YOUR OWN ADVENTURE: MYSTERY OR ROMANCE

MADDIE SWALLOWS MYSTERIES:

New Mexican Cozy Mystery

Dead Before Dinner

Dead Upon Arrival

Dead Before I Do

Dead Among Stars

Dead by Design

Dead in the Dark

Dead Without a Hitch

SEASIDE FRENCH PATISSERIE MYSTERIES

Death and Dacquoise

Poison and Pudding

Bullets and Beignets

BORROWING AMOR: New Mexican Romance

Borrowing Amor

Borrowing Love

Borrowing a Fiancé

Borrowing a Billionaire

ABOUT THE AUTHOR

Kat Bellemore is the author of both the Borrowing Amor small town romance series and the Maddie Swallows cozy mystery series. Deciding to have New Mexico as the setting for these series was an easy choice, considering its amazing sunsets, blue skies and tasty green chile. That, and she currently lives there with her husband and two cute kids. They hope to one day add a dog to the family, but for now, the native animals of the desert will have to do. Though, Kat wouldn't mind ridding the world of scorpions and centipedes. They're just mean.

You can visit Kat at www.kat-bellemore.com.